GREEN EYED
MONSTER

By the Author

Falling Star

Green Eyed Monster

What Reviewers Say About Bold Strokes Books

"With its expected unexpected twists, vivid characters and healthy dose of humor, *Blind Curves* is a very fun read that will keep you guessing." – *Bay Windows*

"In a succinct film style narrative, with scenes that move, a character-driven plot, and crisp dialogue worthy of a screenplay ... the Richfield and Rivers novels are ... an engaging Hollywood mystery ... series." – *Midwest Book Review*

Force of Nature "...is filled with nonstop, fast paced action. Tornadoes, raging fire blazes, heroic and daring rescues... Baldwin does a fine job of describing the fast-paced scenes and inspiring the reader to keep on turning the pages." – *L-word.comLiterature*

In the Jude Devine mystery series the "...characters seem fully capable of walking away from the particulars of whodunit and engaging the reader in other aspects of their lives." – *Lambda Book Report*

Mine "...weaves a tale of yearning, love, lust, and conflict resolution ... a believable plot, with strong characters in a charming setting." – *JustAboutWrite*

"While these two women struggle with their issues, there is some very, very hot sex. If you enjoy complex characters and passionate sex scenes, you'll love *Wild Abandon*." – *MegaScene*

"*Course of Action* is a romance ... populated with a host of captivating and amiable characters. The glimpses into the lifestyles of the rich and beautiful people are rather like guilty pleasures ... a most satisfying and entertaining reading experience." – *Midwest Book Review*

The Clinic is "...a spellbinding novel." – *JustAboutWrite*

"*Unexpected Sparks* lived up to its promise and was thoroughly enjoyable ... Dartt did a lovely job at building the relationship between Kate and Nikki." – *Lambda Book Report*

"*Sequestered Hearts* ... is everything a romance should be. It is teeming with longing, heartbreak, and of course, love. As pure romances go, it is one of the best in print today." – *L-word.comLiterature*

"*The Exile and the Sorcerer* is a mesmerizing read, a tour-de-force packed with adventure, ordeals, complex twists and turns, and the internal introspection of appealing characters." – *Midwest Book Review*

The Spanish Pearl is "...both science fiction and romance in this adventurous tale ... A most entertaining read, with a sequel already in the works. Hot, hot, hot!" – *Minnesota Literature*

"A deliciously sexy thriller ... *Dark Valentine* is funny, scary, and very realistic. The story is tightly written and keeps the reader gripped to the exciting end." – *JustAbout Write*

"*Punk Like Me* ... is different. It is engaging. It is life-affirming. Frankly, it is genius. This is a rare book in that it has a soul; one that is laid bare for all to see." – *JustAboutWrite*

"*Chance* is not a novel about the music industry; it is about a woman discovering herself as she muddles through all the trappings of fame." – *Midwest Book Review*

Sweet Creek "... is sublimely in tune with the times." – *Q-Syndicate*

"*Forever Found* ... neatly combines hot sex scenes, humor, engaging characters, and an exciting story." – *MegaScene*

Shield of Justice is a "...well-plotted...lovely romance...I couldn't turn the pages fast enough!" – Ann Bannon, author of *The Beebo Brinker Chronicles*

The 100th Generation is "...filled with ancient myths, Egyptian gods and goddesses, legends, and, most wonderfully, it contains the lesbian equivalent of Indiana Jones living and working in modern Egypt." – *Just About Write*

Sword of the Guardian is "...a terrific adventure, coming of age story, a romance, and tale of courtly intrigue, attempted assassination, and gender confusion ... a rollicking fun book and a must-read for those who enjoy courtly light fantasy in a medieval-seeming time." – *Midwest Book Review*

"*Of Drag Kings and the Wheel of Fate*'s lush rush of a romance incorporates reincarnation, a grounded transman and his peppy daughter, and the dark moods of a troubled witch—wonderful homage to Leslie Feinberg's classic gender-bending novel, *Stone Butch Blues*." – *Q-Syndicate*

In *Running with the Wind* "...the discussions of the nature of sex, love, power, and sexuality are insightful and represent a welcome voice from the view of late-20-something characters today." – *Midwest Book Review*

"Rich in character portrayal, *The Devil Inside* is an unusual, unpredictable, and thought-provoking love story that will have the reader questioning the definition of right and wrong long after she finishes the book." – *JustAboutWrite*

Wall of Silence "...is perfectly plotted and has a very real voice and consistently accurate tone, which is not always the case with lesbian mysteries." – *Midwest Book Review*

GREEN EYED MONSTER

by

Gill McKnight

2008

GREEN EYED MONSTER
© 2008 BY GILL MCKNIGHT. ALL RIGHTS RESERVED.

ISBN 10: 1-60282-042-2
ISBN 13: 978-1-60282-042-5

THIS TRADE PAPERBACK ORIGINAL IS PUBLISHED BY
BOLD STROKES BOOKS, INC.
P.O. BOX 249
VALLEY FALLS, NY 12185

FIRST EDITION: DECEMBER 2008

CREDITS
EDITOR: CINDY CRESAP
PRODUCTION DESIGN: STACIA SEAMAN
COVER DESIGN BY SHERI (GRAPHICARTIST2020@HOTMAIL.COM)

Acknowledgments

Gracious thanks to my BSB editors, Jennifer, Cindy, and Stacia. And to Sheri for making the cover fun.

To Effy, as always, for her endless encouragement and advice. To Viv, for her energy and support.

And of course, to Ruth, Georgi, Kirstin, and Rae for the beta reading and clever insights. Thanks, guys!

Dedication

For Briege, the original monster, and Ali Bali Bee.
I was the static in your attic.
Thank you for letting me share your home.
Kisses to you both. xxx

CHAPTER ONE

She awoke…well, came around, into blackness. Confused at first, she took a few seconds to note the fabric bound tightly round her eyes and the gag across her mouth. And knots. Knots that lashed her to the chair, stretching her muscles to the screaming point. Disorientation, shock, dismay. *What the fuck?* How had she gotten here? What was happening? Bile rose in her throat as fear rattled through her, blurring all thought, slamming her in the guts. Then her reflexes kicked in. Her personal survival mechanism that she trusted like none other. Her logic, her wits, her innate wisdom. No time to panic, to wonder at circumstance, only time to be smart.

The pounding in her head was pushed aside as she sat and listened as acutely as possible for clues, anything that might help. No breathing, no movement, no anything. Not even the air stirred. No one was there with her, not even sitting quietly. She detected no other presence at all. So what else could she hear? Noise from the outside? Again, nothing. No traffic, no weather, no neighborhood, nothing. She might as well be in a coffin, buried alive.

The chilling thought threw her into irrational horror. Panic and claustrophobia rose to swamp her. She breathed in, deep and slow. One, two, three, four, and hold for five beats, then one, two, three, four, and release. *Repeat as necessary*, she told herself, *until the fear subsides, until your heart calms. Until your wits are back inside your dumb-ass head.*

Several deep breaths later and she had a grip on her panic. That was stupid, she scolded herself. Stop thinking about coffins. Her life might be in danger. Certainly her safety was. She raised her head slightly, letting her nose play detective.

Mmm, oil. Motor oil. And detergent. Yes, dishwashing detergent with a lavender scent. Nothing else. That was it. She was either tied up in someone's garage or maybe a utility room. Great, just great. Now how the hell did this happen?

She'd been in the kitchen at home. Then what? Why was it so hard to recall?

Her head was banging like a drum, as if she had a hangover, but she hadn't been drinking. Had she? *Think. Water.* She remembered sipping water, then— Oh, God. The heart attack! How could she have forgotten the heart attack? But wait a minute. That couldn't have been a heart attack. She'd have woken up in a hospital, not gagged and blindfolded on a chair somewhere.

She'd been drugged and kidnapped. It was so simple, so apparent now. She remembered drinking from the glass, her last act of normality in her own home. And then the palpitations, so strong the tumbler had slipped from her grasp to the floor. She had followed soon after, onto the cool tiles with a wave of sickening dizziness. Her head spinning and heart pumping for all it was worth.

She hazily remembered the back door had opened and someone entered. As the cloying blackness engulfed her, she recalled the relief that someone had arrived who would help her, who would run for help.

The question was, what the hell was she doing here? This wasn't help, this wasn't a hospital, this was trouble. Terrifying trouble.

Time crept by. It was important to quell her fears and not let them overwhelm her. She had to keep her mind occupied, gather clues, remember details, and keep a hold on her panic. When she felt her spirits flag, she rallied, strengthening herself mentally for whatever lay ahead. *Knowledge is power. I am not afraid. Well, not much. I don't know who's grabbed me. I don't know what they want. But the clues I have are expanding by the minute. So relax, breathe deep, use your brain, and help yourself get out of this mess.*

Another of her senses kicked in to add to her growing database of clues. The warm glow of sunshine crept across her shoulder, and with its steady movement she tried to calculate time. Now she knew she had a window somewhere to the left. That meant an outer wall. Whatever the layout of this building was, she was on an outer edge. It confirmed her initial idea of either a garage or utility room. She hoped she was at ground level with just one wall between herself and freedom. If she could free her binds she might have a chance, but struggling proved futile. She was tied too securely. Whoever bound her knew what they were doing. That did not bode well.

Footsteps! She jerked up straighter at the measured pace of footsteps. A soft foot tread came from the right, in another room. She guessed maybe two hours had passed from when she'd regained consciousness, but she had lost the sun some time ago and all sense of daylight hours with it. Even a dripping tap would have given her a unit of measurement. This continual silence distorted all concept of time. The sudden clatter of dishes in a sink confirmed this new arrival was in a kitchen. She was most definitely in a room off a kitchen, but she was still uncertain if it was a garage or the utility room.

The clattering of dishes stopped and was replaced by a low drone and then a ding. A microwave ding. Someone was making dinner. Or lunch? She guessed dinner as the sun had earlier shone with the fading heat of a fall afternoon, but it was only a guess. These little mind games were holding her together by keeping her thoughts slightly left of center and away from her increasing stress. She needed to focus on something other than pure panic.

So, it was dinnertime. Immediately, her stomach started to

rumble. *Well, what do you know?* A vital, clue-filled physical attribute overlooked—her hunger. It could have been her clock if she'd even registered it in the first place. At work, her stomach was her timepiece, pacing her day.

She focused intently on every movement from the adjoining room. Four steps from the microwave to the silverware drawer. Two more steps and a cupboard door snapped open. It sounded like a small kitchen. This felt like a large room; utility rooms were seldom larger than their kitchens, so this was more likely the garage. Another piece of the puzzle fell into place.

Five steps and a connecting door clicked open. The entire acoustics of the room changed. She had company. Ten steps for her visitor to reach her. This was definitely the larger room. Now she smelled the waft of approaching food, and her stomach growled again. Fancifully, she thought she could probably guess the cubic footage of this room from the echoes of her rumbling belly.

Her visitor's footsteps slowed beside her and hesitated. She had the immediate impression of height, but that could have been because she was seated, or because she was feeling intimidated. *It's only an impression*, she told herself. It still had to be proven. Underlying the heady aroma of food lay the warm, soapy scent of a female? Every primal and cognizant instinct in her body told her this was a woman standing beside her. So she had one female captor. How many more were there?

"I heated up some broth. It's vegetable. Wasn't sure if you were vegetarian." The voice was soft and low with a Midwest drawl that in other circumstances she'd have found attractive. "I also got you some water and some painkillers. I'm gonna undo the gag. Please don't holler. There's no one to hear you. And to be honest, if you're difficult, I'll gag you again and take the food away. Understand?"

This was followed by the scrape of a metal tray being set on the floor beside her. Then her captor easily flicked free the gag. *This has to be the person who tied it in the first place.* She grimaced in a fierce cheek stretch, smacked her lips, and licked them with a dry tongue. What a blessed relief.

"Here. Suck this." The plastic nipple of a sports water bottle was gently inserted into her parched mouth.

"Just a few sips at a time." Before she had even drawn her second greedy draught, the bottle was removed.

"Not so fast. You'll make yourself sick." Again, the nipple was carefully introduced and she took another sip.

"Here comes the spoon. Ready?" She listened intently to the simple noises of a spoon dipping in liquid, scraping on the lip of the bowl. Her nostrils flared at the aroma of hot, herby soup. Her stomach gave another appreciative gurgle. And then, out of the blue, an unexpected sound. A long, whispered breath?

What is she doing? Blowing. She's blowing on the spoon. Cooling the soup like you would for a child? Kidnappers didn't do that. Kidnappers cut off your ears and sent them to your loved ones. Maybe this was the minder until the rest of the gang arrived with their knives.

The spoon was prodding her lips. She allowed the broth to trickle into her mouth. It was ambrosia. She had no idea of the last time she'd eaten, but judging by her hunger, it must have been ages ago. Over the next ten minutes the process was repeated until the bowl was emptied.

"You enjoy that?" The voice came again as the bowl was placed back onto the metal tray. A little pulse of—what? Relief?—resonated in it.

"It was good," she said. What came next, the gag? No, no, not that. She didn't think she could bear it. What to do to prolong the moment, to delay the panic, to glean more information?

"Thank you," she continued. *Keep talking. Make a connection. She seems to be kind. Well, kind enough, considering she's a kidnapper.*

"I got some aspirin here. I'm guessing you've got a nasty headache. Do you want some?"

"Aspirin?"

"Yup, aspirin. That's all it is. Promise."

So she *had* been drugged. Definitely something in the water made her pass out. Her head was killing her. Could she trust this woman? Did she want this woman to think she *would* trust her? What was she to make of these attempts at kindness and consideration? How useful were they to her beyond her immediate physical comfort?

"No, thank you. I'd rather not. But I would like some more water, please."

There, a compromise. She wouldn't let her captor think she could just blow away her head pain as easily as she cooled her soup. But she would let her supply the basic needs for her comfort and survival. After all, it was all about trust. The kidnapper seemed to want some; the kidnapped had none to give.

"Sure. Here you go. Ready?" The bottle was quickly reintroduced. It seemed important her modest request was answered, that she be appeased in the small matter of extra fluids. That probably meant feelings of guilt on the part of her kidnapper. Useful information, but what else could she wheedle out of this present situation?

"Are you my minder?"

"Sorry?"

"Are you going to look after me until this is all over?"

"Oh, yeah. It should be all over in a few hours, tops. Then I'll let you go. Don't worry. It'll be quick." There was a desperate cheerfulness in the voice.

Then I'll let you go? So this woman was in charge? Was she acting alone? How had she infiltrated her home and drugged her? And why was she trying so hard to reassure her captive all would be well? God, she felt so fuzzy and slow-witted. On a good day she'd be halfway out the door by now, leaving her captor on the floor all negotiated out. A few more sips of water, and nature came to her aid.

"I really need the bathroom." It was true and it might be useful as long as she wasn't directed toward a bucket in the corner. But somehow she didn't think that was the case. Someone who blew on her broth would hopefully not make her squat over a drain hole.

"Oh, right. Hmm."

The slight hesitancy in the voice alerted her that her captor had not really thought about her sanitary needs. *What kind of half-assed, amateur kidnapper have I got here? C'mon, what did she expect? Feed me, water me, then leave me to explode?*

Or maybe the turnover should have been immediate, was expected to be immediate. So immediate there would have been no need to feed, water, or toilet her captive. *Jesus, has something gone wrong already?* What happened to "all over in a few hours, tops"? She began to feel her initial worry rise, and with it, her panic. Her breath must have caught in her throat, for at once the voice reassured her.

"I'm gonna untie your wrists and guide you. We'll go slow. Just follow my directions."

She was now almost certain this was the only bad guy. Flexing and rotating her newly released fingers and wrists, she stood up cautiously, relieved to have no pins and needles, and no cramps. At least her captor knew how to tie a proper knot. Was she a sailor, or a trucker? Maybe a BDSMer? She mentally shook herself out of her semihysteria.

Her arms were drawn behind, and once more, her wrists bound together. She was pulled in close to her guide's side until she could feel the crush of a soft breast against her shoulder. Yup, she was right. This was a tall one. The warmth of the connection contrasted with the chill in her body, reminding her again that the sun had long disappeared.

"Stay close. I'll guide you." The warm voice reverberated above her head. Then, a clichéd afterthought. "And no funny stuff."

Yes, this whole affair was beginning to smack of rank amateurism, and that was very, very dangerous for her. She wasn't sure how much control her abductor had over the situation. If the last twenty minutes were anything to go by, it seemed pretty tenuous. The sooner she gained some leverage with this person, the better. Situations like this were all about control. She had to wrest some away from this woman, and within the next twenty-four hours, for it to be effective.

She was carefully led across the floor to the connecting doorway. It took fifteen of her shorter steps, more confirmation her captor was indeed taller and with a much longer stride. When they entered what she assumed to be the kitchen, the wave of heat made her skin flush. Left turn, six of her strides to another door, moving from tiles to carpeting, five strides to the left and into a bathroom. The change in acoustics told her this. More tiles underfoot. They stood there awkwardly for several seconds. Now that they'd reached their destination, her captor seemed to have run out of steam.

Now what? Now what indeed, she could almost hear the clunking rattle of her captor's mind. *God, what an idiot. This just gets worse.*

"Are you going to untie me?" Even as she asked, she could feel uncertainty oozing from the other woman.

"No," came her answer. "You might tamper with the blindfold, and I don't want you to see me."

"I won't touch it. Just free my hands so I can use the toilet. Please."

"No." This time the voice was terse. She decided not to push it. They stood in silence.

"Are you going to help me, then?" Her own voice was tight, her face turned in the general direction of her companion. A touch on her shoulder gently guided her backward.

"The bowl is directly behind you." Hands quickly popped her fly buttons, easing her Levi's down to her knees. Tentative fingers fluttered on the elastic of her lace panties before lowering them, too. She felt her face burn. A hand held her shoulder and supported her as she clumsily sat down, leaning forward to awkwardly counterbalance her arms tied behind her. Her mortification was compounded a few minutes later as she heard the toilet tissue rip before its softness brushed against her, tidying her.

"Up we come." The voice was brusque and embarrassed.

She was pulled to her feet and her clothing rearranged. Again, she felt like a small child, first spoon-fed, now potty trained. *Why is she putting us both through this embarrassment? It's excruciating. I hate it. It's got to stop, somehow.*

Leaving the bathroom, she was again guided out into the corridor. This time they turned away from where they'd originally come. She was being taken farther into the building. Good, another segment of the floor map could be pasted into her head. Garage/utility, kitchen, corridor, bathroom. It was all building up nicely. If she ever got a run for it, she at least stood half a chance of finding an exit, blindfolded or not.

A door opened. She was maneuvered through and brought to a halt. Though still nervous and vulnerable on one level, on another, her intuition was feeding her courage and confidence. Already, she had the measure of her captor, and this one was no professional. Perhaps she could work that to her own advantage; a lot depended on how the rest of the abduction played out. A speedy release was imperative. She needed to get out of here as soon as possible.

"You'll sleep here. The gar—the other room is chilly." She was nudged to sit on the edge of a bed. Her abductor moved away and she heard a drawer open, followed by the clinking of metal. The ties were again undone, freeing her hands.

"Lie down." She was pressed back onto the pillows. A click, and cold metal cuffed her wrists before her. Her arms were pulled over her head, and the cuffs were then looped to the railed headboard with rope, giving her some maneuverability, but not much. Next, she felt her sneakers and socks being peeled off and a blanket drawn up to her waist.

"Tell me why you're doing this. Is it for money?"

"No." The answer was quick and a little too sharp. Silence. "Well, yeah. But only what's mine."

"What do you mean only what's yours? Why have you brought me here? I don't understand."

"You don't have to understand. All you have to do is exactly as you're told. It'll be over soon. I already started negotiations with your girlfriend."

"My girlfriend? What's she got to do with it? What's going on here?"

"Yeah. It won't be long till Victoria Gresham pays back what she owes me, and you'll be free."

She started in shock. The metal chain of the cuffs rattled. Before she could even think to speak, she heard her abductor move toward the doorway.

"I'm leaving the door open. I'll be down the hall. Call if you need anything." Then she was gone with a soft, "Good night, Ginette."

CHAPTER TWO

Eventually, she slept, which surprised her when she awakened later with her head still spinning. She thought she was going to scream with the frustration of it all but talked herself down from the precipice and focused instead on the information her captor had casually imparted. At least she now had an appreciation of the situation. The more she knew, the better chance she had of escaping. Maybe she could find a way to use her captor and get free.

"Good morning, Ginette. I got breakfast all ready. Come on. Let's do the bathroom thing first."

The voice seemed more confident this morning. The cuffs were released from the bed and her wrists captured behind her back again. No shoes this time. Barefoot, she was led to the bathroom, the reverse direction confirming the floor map she was building in her mind. She was turned at the bowl. Her Levi's buttons were opened, this time with more assurance.

"Do you have to humiliate me like this? Can't you let me use the bathroom by myself?"

The bitch was beginning to get off on this now that the first-night nerves were over. It was essential to be firm but careful. The next few hours were important. She would emerge as either the psychological victim or victor, and she knew which one she wanted to be. Even as the thought entered her head, she felt the hands on her hips hesitate. Her captor was obviously wavering. Maybe she wasn't so complacent with the situation after all.

"I suppose, but there's rules. If I leave you alone, promise there'll be no tampering with the blindfold, okay?"

There was doubt in the question, so she nodded quickly to reassure. She was surprised that the woman had backed down in their first test of wills. No more humiliating nursemaid games.

"I mean it." Her captor seemed to realize she'd shown weakness, growling, "You tamper, and it'll be the sorriest thing you ever did. Got that?" A key click, and her hands were freed from the cuffs.

"Yes, no tampering." Hopefully, that sounded cowed and obedient. "I understand. Thank you." *Thank you for pretending I'm human, you bastard.*

"Okay." The voice withdrew toward the door. "I'm just outside. The tissue is beside you, the soap and towel by the basin. And the window is wired shut. Don't do anything stupid. I'm taking a big chance here, Ginette. Don't let me down."

The door clicked shut, and her lunatic attacker did not seem to be lurking in the room to test her. When there was no sound for a minute or more, she pushed up a corner of the blindfold and saw a standard, nondescript bathroom. Sighing with relief, she tested the window. It was wired shut, as her abductor had promised, and if the view was any indication, they were in a cabin in the middle of nowhere. If she broke out, where the hell would she run?

She took a look inside the cabinet. Unfortunately, no Mace. A roll-on deodorant. Maybe she could throw it at her captor's head? Cotton balls, hand cream. Nail clippers. Forbidden in the cabin of a plane, so they had to be dangerous somehow?

She grimaced. Her humor was slipping as rapidly as her sanity, and her time was almost up. She closed the mirrored door and completed her bathroom business in double time, pulling the blindfold back into position before calling out, "Ready."

"You tampered with this." Angry fingers jerked the knot tighter.

"Ouch, you're hurting me."

"I told you not to touch it." Her kidnapper sounded agitated.

"I dropped the soap and couldn't find it. I had to take a peek. Look, I pulled it back into position. Believe me, I really don't want to see you. I'll have bad enough nightmares after this without your face being in them."

The blindfold was tested with a rough pull that caught her hair. Her nerve began to falter. She couldn't bear it if her captor was going to be sadistic. The freak could flip out and kill her at any moment, for all she knew.

"Please stop. Does it have to be so tight?"

"You have only yourself to blame," her tormentor replied.

"I see. You're getting off on this. It's a power trip." The words spilled out in a rush of fear and anger before she could censor them. She caught at her breath, terrified that her stress had caused such a dangerous outburst.

How were people supposed to behave in situations like this so they would survive? She was confident in dealing with most opponents, but some lunatic who'd snatched her from her own home? How could she relate to a mindset like that? She drew a steadying breath and tried to redirect her thoughts along a more positive track. Hey, she'd won the right to pee alone. That was major. And her abductor didn't even seem to know she'd lost the first important skirmish.

When the hands returned, promising more pain, she said hastily, "I'm sorry. I didn't mean that."

Instead, a modicum of slack entered the blindfold knot, relieving the hateful pinching.

"The sooner you're outta here, the better," said her captor.

❖

Once she was seated in the kitchen, the aroma of fresh coffee and bacon felt comforting and lifted her spirits.

"Okay, Ginette. I got eggs, bacon, pancakes, or just cereal if you like? What's it to be? What can I get you?"

"Your name would be good." She took a chance.

"I can't do that."

"I need to call you something. White slaver? Human trafficker? How about Snatch?"

"How's your headache? Do you need any painkillers?" Okay, so her attempts at humor were going to be ignored. Pity, people gave away so many clues through jocularity.

"You mean after you just hauled half my head off?" She decided to go for guilt, as humor wasn't getting her any leverage. It worked.

"Hey, I know you're caught up in the middle of a bad situation. I know you're completely innocent. I'm trying to make it as easy as I can for you."

The defensive whine tinged with self-justification was infuriating. To hell with censorship, she wanted to rip the head off this mewling jerk. Didn't she realize what she'd put her "victim" through? The shock, the stress, the sheer terror?

"You *kidnapped* me. How easy on me is that?"

"I already acknowledged you were innocent."

"Innocent of what, for fuck's sake?"

"Hey, watch your mouth. You can be gagged again."

"Yes, threaten and bully me, you…you kidnapper. The least you can do is tell me why I'm here and how long until I can go free."

Silence.

Shit. Had she pushed too far? Was the gag going to reappear? That would be a total step backward. She crammed her rage back down, deep inside. Nobody, especially this incompetent amateur, was going to keep her there any longer than necessary.

"Mickey. Call me Mickey." It seemed an impasse had been broken. Again, guilt seemed to be the trigger with Mickey. That was very useful to know.

"Thank you, Mickey. That wasn't too hard, now was it?" Another victory. So what if it was a fake name? Given enough time, she could wrangle "Mickey's" favorite grade school teacher out of her. The more Mickey talked, the more she revealed herself. Her levels of competence were incredibly low for a felon. A smart captive could work her, unsettle her, then soothe her. Keep her off tilt and hope she spilled even more information.

"How long until I can go free?" she asked again.

"That depends on how quickly your girlfriend answers my demands," Mickey replied.

"Which are?"

"None of your business."

"Hey, you're the one treating me like currency. The least you can do is tell me my market value."

This time her outburst didn't gain her anything.

"So what do you want for breakfast? I can make you some oatmeal if you want."

"No. I'm on a hunger strike until you tell me why I'm here." Just then her stomach growled like a grizzly.

"Humph." She could hear humor buried deep in Mickey's voice. "Wonder how that will go? Should be a long, hard fast."

She bristled with anger. "I mean it."

"I'm sure you do. I really believe you're one determined little lady. But trust me, the less you know, the better. I'm gonna have some bacon with my pancakes. And a fresh cup of coffee. So if you'll excuse me, I'll just take you back to the chair in the gara—other room."

"No. I don't want to go back there and just sit. Please, Mickey." She deliberately used the name.

"Well then, if you want to stay here, you gotta eat. Damned if I'm listening to that belly growling at me all day." Mickey got up and began banging pots and pans around on the stove. Water ran from a faucet into a kettle. "I like my coffee strong. Can I get you a cup?" The hunger strike was over.

Breakfast meant more infantilism as she was fork-fed small pieces of food with sips of juice and coffee. Mouth always agape for the next morsel, she felt like a baby bird.

"Boy, you can sure pack it away." Crumbs were judiciously dusted from her lips and chin with a paper napkin. "Now, I have to go to work."

"What? You're leaving me chained up here alone like some dog? Why don't you just tie me up in the backyard, for God's sake?"

"Hey, don't freak out. I work from home, in the back offi— never mind. Look, I'm taking you back to your bedroom and I'll put on some music for you, okay? I promise I won't leave you tied you up in the garage again—damn."

Oh boy, got myself a real rocket scientist here. "I already guessed it was a garage."

"I didn't expect it to take so long," came the sullen reply. "Thought you'd be here and gone in thirty seconds flat. I didn't know where to put you."

Mickey sounded upset that things weren't running smoothly. It seemed she had stupidly brought her captive to her own home, and now she was getting too caught up in the details of caring for her. Probably down to a massive guilt complex. She absolutely stank at criminality. *Interesting. I might just slide out of this in one piece yet.*

"I'll go back to the bedroom, but please don't keep my arms behind my back. My shoulders are killing me."

"All right, but I still have to cuff you to the bed. I don't want you playing with your blindfold again."

She was led back to the room she'd slept in, smiling inwardly. She had memorized the route so well she could do it blindfolded. *How ironic. I am blindfolded.*

Both hands were again cuffed to the bedhead and an MP3 player placed near her head.

"Here's some nice, relaxing music. I'll be just down the hallway. Call me if you need anything, okay?"

❖

Ten minutes later she was screeching over the wail of pan pipes, "If you don't come in here and turn off this godawful noise, I swear I'll inhale my own vomit."

Click! There was blessed silence.

"Oh, thank God," she breathed into the pillow.

"I love pan pipes. How could you not love pan pipes? They're so relaxing." Mickey's hurt voice floated above her.

"You are one sadistic bitch. Do you know that? Are you trying to torture me as well as hold me for ransom?"

"What? Never." Mickey sounded genuinely hurt. "Well, what do you want to listen to? I'm sort of esoteric. I got *Song of the Whales*, *Song of the Dolphins*, *Meditative Wind Chimes*—"

"You *meditate*? Again, I puke in the general direction of my lungs. What I want is an audio book. Do you have anything like that?"

"No. No audio books." Mickey seemed put out she had not availed of her soothing, chilled-out music library. "But I could duck out and get one. Any author in particular?"

"Don't you dare leave me here. What if there's a fire?"

"There won't be a fire. I have to go out sometimes. I need to do chores, like buy milk and bread, collect ransoms, pay bills—"

"Collect ransoms. You're collecting my ransom? How much? When? How?" She tried to sit up, but her cuffs rattled, keeping her prone. She tried to lever herself into a more comfortable position.

"Here, hang on and I'll loosen those." She felt cool, clean breath on her face as Mickey leaned across her to loosen the cuffs. "No. No ransom paying as of yet. But soon. Hopefully, very soon."

Soft, long hair tickled her cheek smelling of bergamot and rosemary, and making her belly flutter, making her want something. She wanted something. She wanted something. She wanted what?

"I want a shower. I'm lying here smelling myself. There must be some way you can let me wash properly."

The slight hesitation from above allowed her to press home her advantage.

"Come on. I'm sweaty and uncomfortable, and all my muscles ache. Please."

"What about the blindfold? You really, really can't see me."

"What is this, a Beauty and the Beast thing?"

"Huh? No! It's a pointing me out in court thing." Her voice was petulant again.

God, but she is so easy to tease. "Look, lock me in the bathroom again and don't let me out until I promise to blindfold myself."

Silence.

"Please, I'll even squirt soap in my eyes."

A chuckle floated down toward her. *Good, she's in a good mood. Just push it a little bit more.* "I'd really appreciate it."

"Let me think about it. Look, I want this to work out for both of us. I know it's tough on you, but I just want us to get through this as easy as possible."

So it's "us" now? Suddenly we're a team trying to get ourselves through this? Oh, darling, I have news for you. There's only ME, and MEAT in my team.

"Please? I'm tired and stinky and achy. No amount of painkillers will make me smell nice. Come on. Give me a break?" She decided to try to play on Mickey's good humor. It worked. More chuckles.

"Okay, I'll go get the bathroom ready. But you have to abide by the rules. Believe me, Ginette, it's important."

CHAPTER THREE

I'm not risking leaving you alone after last time, so you're having a bath, not a shower." Mickey uncuffed her from the bed. She was led to the warm and steamy bathroom.

"Get your clothes off and I'll get you some fresh ones."

Self-consciously, she stepped out of her jeans and panties and pulled her T-shirt over her head. She wore no bra. The day of her kidnapping she had been lolling around the house finishing off a few bits and pieces of office work, and had dressed in her favorite faded Levi's and an old T-shirt. Now she felt so exposed, standing there vulnerable and naked, not knowing if her kidnapper was looking at her. Perhaps Mickey was not even noticing or caring.

In her permanent blindfolded state, she was becoming hypersensitive to Mickey. Her movements, tone of voice, the implied meaning in that soft twang. She was trying to understand every little nuance so she could decode her, undo the riddle of the woman who had seized her and then spent time and effort trying to make up for it.

It surprised her she even cared about Mickey's reaction to her body. It had been a long, long time since she had thought about herself in a sexual manner. To do so now must be her subconscious's way of coping with her current state of vulnerability, to eroticize it, to try to compensate for her loss of real power.

"Be careful as you step in."

A hand took hers and led her to the edge of the tub where she cautiously stepped into perfectly heated water. No sooner had she gingerly lowered herself than one wrist was cuffed to the safety hand bar on the side of the bath. Her other was left free.

"I'm going to wash your hair. I got real nice shampoo and conditioner here. Then I'll leave you alone to wash the rest of yourself and wallow or whatever. Shout when you're done and I'll come back and help you out."

"Okay."

No sooner had she said the word than the blindfold was removed and warm water began to pour from a pitcher soaking her head. Mickey kept out of sight behind her.

It felt so good. Her hair was thoroughly soaked, and the same aromatic shampoo she'd smelled on Mickey was applied. Gentle hands began to massage the suds through her short hair and flit across the tight muscles of her scalp. She bit back a little moan of contentment as the fragrance and the kneading fingers worked their magic on her tension. She didn't want to reward Mickey by letting her know how much she was loving this. It had been so long since she'd been pampered outside of a clinically officious spa.

Again, warm water flowed over her, washing away the lather only for a second application to begin. Firm fingers worked from her crown to the base of her hairline and hesitated for a moment before continuing to knead and massage down to her nape and across her stiff shoulders. This time she could not suppress a long, satisfied moan. She was only human, after all, and this was so delicious.

"You're very tight all across here. Not surprising in the circumstances, I suppose, but I can loosen the muscles up nicely now that the water and steam have relaxed you a little."

"Do you do this for all your kidnap victims?" A little sigh escaped.

She received a warm chuckle. "Oh yeah, some of them feel so pampered I have to chase them out the door."

"Oh, so you're a serial kidnapper. What do you do? Work for the mob?"

This was greeted with a derisive snort. "No way would I want to do this for a living. You're hard enough work as it is."

More water rinsed her hair clean. Then a heavenly scented conditioner was applied and briskly worked into every hair from root to tip.

"This stuff is great for your hair. It sure smells good, too." Mickey seemed to be enjoying the experience.

"You're good at this. Are you a hairdresser, then? I mean when you're not snatching people off the streets?" Best not waste the moment in idle luxury when more information could be wrung from this intimate and informal setting. She was already successfully breaking down Mickey's sorry little boundaries.

Another laugh echoed around the bathroom. "No. Just wanted you to feel a little fresher is all. You've got lovely hair. It's an easy length to work with, I mean," she finished a little awkwardly.

So it was fair to say Mickey's chosen line of work was a million miles away from the hair and beauty industry, despite a natural ability with her hands. Which, of course, was unimportant information and should be disregarded. *Such a nice touch, though.*

A final rinse left her hair feeling refreshed and squeaky clean. Already, she felt like a million-dollar ransom. She congratulated herself on her own cliché. Behind her, she heard Mickey dry her hands on a towel, and to her surprise, move around in front of her, despite her blindfold being removed. She looked up to see a tall, dark blond, and very curvaceous Mickey Mouse. Blazing blues peeked out from the eyeholes in the plastic kid's mask.

"Well, Mickey, so we meet again," she drawled. "The last time was at Cinderella's Castle. I believe I was ten years old. I still have the photograph, and I fully intend to hand it over to the authorities once I'm free. You'll be hunted down like the rat you are."

"Squeak," came the response, accompanied with a mischievous flash from behind the plastic eyeholes.

"So why the hell can't you wear that all day and let me go without a freakin' blindfold?" she demanded, annoyed at the obvious simplicity of her suggestion.

"Because it's too sweaty and my nose gets a heat rash. Now wash yourself with your free hand and call when you want out. There's loads of hot water, so feel free to top up the bath."

Mickey turned and left, leaving the door open. Every inch of her long, denim-clad legs, her broad back gliding down to a trim waist, and her gorgeous curvy butt was ogled on the way out. *Nice, very nice. In the police lineup, I'll get to look at a long line of big, beautiful bottoms.* She began to lather her shoulders, singing at the top of her lungs a cavalcade of popular Disney tunes.

❖

A few yards up the hallway, Mickey sat hunched over her PC in the back bedroom-cum-office, groaning at the off-key refrain. Her captive was proving to be more of a handful than expected, at a time when she needed to concentrate on the complexities of her plan. This little lady's orders just kept rolling in. Mickey was beginning to feel like a short-order chef.

An hour later, the bath had been topped off four times. How long did it take to get clean? Even seals came out of the water to bask sometimes. Glowering at the screen, Mickey was unable to concentrate for more than five minutes at a time.

"Mickeee, the knots you tie are trickeee." Splash, splash,

splash. The shameless butchering of Disney tunes had been going on forever, and now it seemed she was making her up own songs.

I'm gonna drown her! I don't care about the money, I'm gonna drown her. Flinching at a particularly jarring note, she frowned even deeper over her reading glasses. All the attention she had been struggling to give to a particularly complex financial maneuver shattered with a lusty call from the bathroom.

"Mickeee, there's no more hot water."

With a heavy sigh, Mickey rolled back her desk chair, dumped her glasses, and pulled the mask down over her face. On the way to the bathroom she picked up clean boxers and a T-shirt from the bedroom dresser. *This is worse than having a toddler. She was crazy to think this would ever work.*

The song started up again. "Mickeee, Mickeee, Mic—"

Mickey burst into the saturated bathroom and bellowed in sheer exasperation at a morning's work totally lost. "If you don't shut up, I'm leaving you in there till you're a prune."

Silence ensued as her yell echoed off the tiled walls. Big green eyes looked up at her through a tufted fringe of snow blond hair. The naked little body with knees pulled up tight in the name of decorum glowed pink and wet.

She's adorable sitting there like a little water sprite. Shit! Where did that thought come from? She is not adorable. She's a total pain in the ass.

"Well, hello to you, too. Can I get out now please? The water's getting cold."

Mickey set down the clean clothing and pulled the key from her pocket. She released the cuffs from the bath handle.

"I'm gonna let you dress yourself. I'll be in the hall with the door open, so don't go getting any smart ideas, okay? The window is locked."

"Okay, perv," she muttered under her breath.

"Hey. I heard that. I'm *not* a perv."

"Yeah, lurking outside ladies' bathrooms wearing a Mickey Mouse mask." She imitated Mickey's Midwest drawl perfectly. "Fersure you're no perv."

❖

Lunch was another culinary success. Mickey was a serious cook, and her efforts were much appreciated by her captive audience.

"Mmm, that pasta was the greatest." She groaned, patting her little round belly with hands cuffed before her. Mickey was pleased her cooking was so enthusiastically enjoyed, but shook her head at the empty serving dishes. Usually a feast like this would have lasted her two, maybe three days. Her "guest" would eat her out of house and home in no time if something didn't happen soon.

"I've never seen anyone eat as much as you do for your size. You must have more stomachs than a cow." Mickey rose to stack the dishes.

Scraping the plates clean before stashing them in the sink, she watched the blindfold head tilt slightly to try to peek out from under the fabric.

"In case you're interested, I tied it special so you can't see a thing." Mickey knew she sounded smug but didn't regret it. "So just sit still. Wouldn't want you running away straight into a tree. Might dent it." She chuckled.

It was a lovely fall afternoon. Warm sunshine poured through the window, a light breeze and the sound of birdsong wafted in through the open door.

"Hello there." Out of the blue, a man's voice called from outside.

They both froze.

Mickey guessed who it was, and at breakneck speed bolted across the floor. In one leap, she straddled her captive's lap. She took her captive's cuffed hands and thrust them up her sweatshirt out of sight. Mickey's hands meshed in her soft blond hair, covering as much of the blindfold as possible.

She had only one chance at this. She hoped the rental agency guy would head off when he saw she was "busy."

"What the—oh. Oh." Her captive's shocked cry was mumbled into her top. Mickey had to somehow stop her from crying out. With a swooping kiss, she covered the spluttering mouth, sealing off all sound. Tethered hands nudged against the sway of her breasts, a knuckle accidentally grazed her nipple. Her mouth hummed with the angry squawks pouring into it. Mickey did the only thing she could do, she went deep and French, to stopper the garbled squeaking.

With relief, she watched the man's retreat. He would probably come back some other time to check that she was happy with the rental cabin. By then she hoped this nightmare would be over. So far, she'd been lucky. The blindfold and cuffs weren't visible, and she'd moved fast enough to stop a holler for help. Even now, she could feel the indignant tongue quivering against her own in a series of squeaked cursing.

It surprised Mickey how reluctant she was to break the seal, to pull away and release her hold on the pretty face. The muffled squawks continued, but Mickey found her own mouth acting independently of her. It began with sucking on soft lips, running her pliant tongue along the soft inner tissue. Gently, she nipped a lower lip, then stroked it with the tip of her tongue, falling deeper into a truly breathtaking kiss. The protestations beneath her mouth stilled for a surprised second.

Mickey's breasts were warm and flushed. They always did that. It was her embarrassing telltale. She was tantalizingly aware of the cool hands nestling between them. The flush scorched up her neck, heating her cheeks. It happened when she was turned on. *Turned on? Yes, yes, I am. Very, very turned on.*

It amazed her that she should feel this way. How wrong

it was. How wrong to feel attraction to her captive. Stockholm Syndrome, wasn't it? But surely it was supposed to be the other way around, her captive fixating on her? *Oh God, don't tell me I can't even get Stockholm Syndrome right.*

Her state of arousal honestly acknowledged, she was now acutely conscious of the potent little woman humming into her mouth like a very angry bee. After the initial shock, it seemed her captive had regained her righteous indignation and needed to vent. She reluctantly released the swollen lips, freeing the torrent of outrage she had so delightfully corked. And she knew she deserved every word of it. She had definitely taken advantage of the circumstances. Carefully, Mickey pushed the cuffed hands out from under her top and stood up, ready for incoming fire.

"What the hell was that? How dare you. How dare you maul me. Get your hands off. I swear if you so much as touch—"

"Get over it. It was necessary. I didn't see him coming until the last second, or believe me, you'd have been gagged and back in that garage faster than a blink."

"Necessary, my ass. Why were my hands stuffed up your sweater, freako?"

"To hide your cuffs, Einstein. I ain't joking about that garage either. Want to go visit it for a few hours? It's nice and cold. Might cool you off a little." *Why am I defending myself to Little Miss Razor Wire? I'm the damned kidnapper!*

"Don't you threaten me, you…you groper."

"Hey. You're the one who groped me, remember?"

"I never did. You made me. You shoved—"

"Enough." Mickey threw a hand up to halt the onslaught before realizing that her blindfolded captive could not witness the grand gesture. "I'm putting you back in your room. I got work to do, and *you* can lie quietly for once and listen to that audio book I downloaded for you. And if I hear so much as one *peep*, I swear it's a gag and the garage for you. Got it?"

Mickey needed to sit down at her computer and get lost in

the only world she understood and was master of. She had to completely remove herself from the madness this little madam always managed to promote in her, if only for one blessed hour of peace. Grabbing an arm, she bundled her fuming detainee back up the hall. Still very shaken after the close call, Mickey had to sit and think. She had to reformulate her kidnap plans. And whether she cared to admit it or not, process that unexpected kiss.

CHAPTER FOUR

Mickey had stomped off to do whatever it was she did in the back room, leaving her captive tethered to the bed to contemplate their bizarrely interrupted afternoon.

Her skin flushed at the memory of the heated softness of Mickey's breasts, her tied hands nestling in that silken valley. It had been an extremely pleasant, mind-numbing sensation. And along with that blazer of a kiss, totally corrupting. Enough to blow the only opportunity for rescue she was ever likely to get.

It was aggravating beyond words that her logic had been so easily derailed by a kiss and a pair of boobs—all tossed out the window in one breathtaking moment.

No, she couldn't dwell on it anymore. She had to escape, free herself. It was too confusing and distracting, all these thoughts and feelings were rampaging through her like a hormone derby. Her hormones were obviously out of control. It had been months since she'd been sexual. She snorted to herself. And what a fiasco that had been. Lesbian bed death, rigor mortis, and private funeral had all passed through her bedroom at alarming speed. *In lieu of flowers, please send donations to my vibrator fund.*

She groaned. She was horny. So did not need this. *Not now, for God's sake. Not here under these crazy conditions.*

❖

"Ginette? Can I ask you something?" The MP3 player was switched off and the weight of another body tilted the edge of the mattress.

"Victoria Gresham, your girlfriend. She *is* around, isn't she? I mean, she's not off traveling or anything, is she?"

"What do you mean?"

"Well, you see…"

"No, I don't see. What do you mean?" Something was wrong.

"I mean, well…"

"What the fuck do you mean?"

A short silence. The expletive seemed to jar Mickey before she continued.

"She isn't answering my e-mails. You two are getting along, aren't you?"

"Your e-mails?"

"Yeah, I have her private e-mail address, and I've been sending my demands directly to her, but she's ignoring me. Something ain't right." A deep, pained sigh followed. "How well were you two getting along before I kidnapped you?"

"Wait. You're sending *e-mails* as ransom demands? How the hell can you make sure they're not traceable? What about your IP?"

Mickey was clearly taken aback. "Hey, I'm in the business. I can cope. Nothing comes back on me that I don't want."

"Oh, so you're a geek? A hacker who sees her technical abilities as a right to operate outside the law of digitally challenged folks."

"I am not a hacker. I am a bona fide developer." Mickey unintentionally gave up another clue as she defended herself.

"What exactly do you mean, 'her private e-mail'?" she continued relentlessly now that she had her abductor off balance. "Where exactly have you been sending these demands to?"

An e-mail address was reeled off to her that made her heart

turn cold. She knew no one would be picking up on that mailbox. It was private, all right; practically redundant, in fact. Used only for domestic purposes, never business, just shopping and vacation planning, and no one would be opening it soon. *Shit, this crazy woman's ransom demands are bouncing off into the ether. I could be tied up here until my eightieth birthday!*

"Well, try another one, for God's sake. I can't wait around all day for monies to be exchanged. I need to get out of here." Panic crept into her voice, though she tried to quell it. On hearing it, a warm, reassuring hand reached out to rest just above her knee. The suddenness of the touch on her bare thigh below her boxers startled her, and her cuffs clanked against the bedrails. The hand instantly withdrew.

"I did. I tried yours. I figured once she noticed you were gone, the first thing she'd do is check your mail."

"Mine?"

"Yup. Ginette.Felstrom@Greshamcorps.com. Hey, you may think I'm a bumbler, but I'm pretty damned smart. Smart enough to have my intellectual copyright stolen by *your* girlfriend and her Gresham Corporation."

Oh, this sounds bad. Very bad. This whole kidnapping is a disaster. Perhaps I can convince her to let me go. Bribe her or something...get her sympathy...

"Did she steal from you, Mickey?" She tried to sound sincere yet shocked.

"Are you being sarcastic? She's your girlfriend. Everyone knows she's a premenstrual piranha. And yeah, she stole my idea. My code." Mickey's voice rose with indignation. "This was the perfect plan. The perfect revenge and get even. Except nobody's listening to me." Her voice rang with self-righteousness. "It should've taken less than three hours, tops, and here we are, day two. Are you sure she's not outta town or something? I mean, why isn't she climbing the walls looking for you?"

"Well, actually, we split up."

"What?" A stupefied bellow.

"We split up. Separated. Broke up." Her litany was almost gleeful as she sensed waves of panic rolling from Mickey's body. "Ended our relationship. Went separate ways. Fell out of love. Had an emotional meltdown. Needed space. Took time out. Divor—"

"What?" More like a stupefied squeak now. This news had obviously knocked Mickey clear out of the ballpark.

"I'd love to see your face right now. I'm sure it's a picture."

"It's a fucking Van Gogh."

"Look, Mickey, why don't you just let me go? You're not a killer. You're not even a very good kidnapper. Break even while you still can. Drive me into the wilds and dump me. Let me find my own way home. Like Lassie."

Her words where met with silence, though she could have sworn she heard the unlubricated cogs in Mickey's brain rustily turning as she tried to come up with an alternative strategy. So the kidnapper had no contingency plans and was now confused.

Holding back a smile, she put her considerable powers of persuasion to work. "Please, Mickey. No one is looking for me. They'll all think I've dropped out to nurse a broken heart." She paused for effect before croaking out, "No one misses me or cares enough to pay a ransom." Damned blindfold. She could have squeezed out convincing tears, given half a chance.

"Shit, I've got to think," Mickey finally muttered. She rose and released the cuffs from the headboard, then locked them to the front, as was becoming her habit.

"C'mon. Dinner time. I can hear your belly gurgling already." Mickey sighed, mumbling absently as she led her from the room. "I made us a nice casserole for tonight."

This time she was led to the kitchen by a large hand cupping her bound ones. It felt warm and secure, and it brought a small smile to her lips. *Hmm, holding hands now, are we? Isn't this cozy?* Cozy and interesting. So, someone had no backup plan, and someone was hanging on to her now? The tide was finally turning.

Out loud she asked, "What kind of casserole? Chicken?"

❖

"You sound remarkably cheerful about breaking up." Mickey's glum voice drifted over the table toward her. "Sounds like you're glad to be rid of her."

"Trust me, I have never missed Victoria Gresham's checkbook so much in my entire life, thanks to you. Ever thought of couples therapy? You'd make a fortune with your uniquely radical approach."

"What was it like?" Mickey asked.

"Are you asking about the experience of being kidnapped? Let me see—"

"No, what was it like being with her? Victoria Gresham. I mean, she's one of the top five hundred wealthiest women in the country. They say negotiating with her is like walking a high wire over your own open grave. So what was it like being her partner?"

Tonight's meal was hands free, a hard-won victory. The other bonus was the obvious froth Mickey was in at the news of her single white female status.

"It was like any relationship. We slept, ate, worked, relaxed together. Money doesn't make people love each other any better. Sure, we could afford whatever we wanted, but work always came first. It has to, to have that sort of income, so there's no quality time, and your relationship suffers." She grew flustered as she felt pushed to defend...what? A privileged lifestyle? Another failed relationship? She'd worked damn hard to feel this empty.

"Sounds *real* romantic. Money and love—the American dream." Mickey snorted.

"Well, you seem invested for at least fifty percent."

Mickey ignored the jibe. "So why did you split up?"

"You know, I was joking about the couples therapy thing. I really don't want to talk about it."

"No, tell me. What happened?"

"Why are you asking this? No answer I give is going to get you your money. Give it up and let me go. You suck at kidnapping. Just accept it."

"Tell me."

She sighed, deciding to plow on and answer the questions, unsure where they would lead or what Mickey hoped to learn. Maybe her captor just needed to accept the inevitable: it was over. All of it was over. Her relationship, along with Mickey's glorious revenge plans, had spun out, derailed, and now lay in a ditch, smoking. Now she had to somehow persuade Mickey to think about damage control, loss limitation, and letting her go.

"We simply didn't love each other enough. Not for a long time. But sometimes the heart's a little slow to confess. Sometimes it just craves that cozy old comfort zone, and you end up going through the motions, like a tired old dance." She suddenly, unexpectedly, found herself being honest. "Okay, it was simple, really. She was bored. She stopped loving me a long time ago. But she just kept hanging on."

"Out of habit? That comfort zone thing?"

"Something like that."

"What about you? Are you still in love with her?"

"No. I'm guilty of the same sins. But at least I did break my habit eventually and ended it between us. Now my heart's in withdrawal."

"When did you stop loving her?"

"As soon as…as soon as I met my replacement."

"Who was your replacement?"

"You mean *what* was my replacement. Money. She simply loved the money more." As quickly as she'd opened up, she closed down again. She didn't like the direction of this conversation but couldn't put her finger on the moment she'd lost control of it.

Why all these questions? What use could they be? Idle curiosity? Panicked plotting? Where was Mickey going with this?

"So what are you going to do now that I'm worthless? Kill me?" She decided to force Mickey to look at the cold consequences. "If you're not prepared to free me, what else is there? Have you really thought this through? Because one thing I'll literally bet my life on is you're no killer." *Jeez, you're barely a competent criminal.*

"You're not worthless. You're never that." Mickey's voice sounded suspiciously lighter. Had she gleaned something from the intimate conversation? Quickly, she returned to business. "But why is she not answering the e-mails? What the hell is she up to?"

❖

"I can't believe you're putting me to bed early, like some toddler. I've done nothing but lie on that freaking bed all day. I'll get bedsores."

"It's not early. It's late. Now shut up and go to sleep. I got tons of work to catch up on."

"It's not even dark. This blindfold doesn't shut out the light, you know. It must be only eight o'clock at the latest."

"Just can it, okay?" Mickey was not going to be swayed. "Get back into bed this minute. I'll leave the radio on. You can listen to *Late Nite Chatline* if you're good."

"*Late Nite Chatline*? That won't start for a million years. It's the middle of the day, remember?"

"Christ, you're one moaning little bitch. You'll listen to whatever's on, okay? Now shut up. I got work to do."

"Hey," she whined, shaking her cuffs against the bed rail. "Please? Cut me some slack? Just enough to scratch my nose or change radio channels?"

"The blindfold—"

"Does it matter that much now that you have the mask?

Please, Mickey, I promise not to take it off. Just one hand free, please? Please?" Silence greeted her pleas. *Good, she's thinking about it. Sucker.*

"No."

"What!"

"No. I can't trust you not to mess with the blindfold again. I can't risk you seeing me. Sorry, kiddo, no can do."

"Nooooo. My arms are going to fall off, my shoulders are killing me, my neck hurts, my tummy's—"

"Oh, for crying out loud. Look, I'll lengthen this tether by a few inches. Okay? I'll set the radio right up close to your hand on the bedside table right here. You can reach the buttons now. Hit enough of them and you can figure out the stations." This was explained with what sounded like a smile. "Now I gotta go to work. I'll check in on you later. Okay?"

She lay there glowering.

"Yes, okay," she grumbled at the retreating footsteps. Dammit. She wanted a free hand, a hairpin, and a minute to work on the cuffs—then voila! Freedom. It always worked like that in the movies. But then the movies didn't have a big, stupid, doofus to spoil the script.

The *Late Nite Chatline* show was a favorite, and she might as well try to catch it. She'd been on an easy listening channel most of the evening, but now she wanted to hear human voices and find out what was going on in the world outside. Though for her, it felt like she was tuning in from another planet.

Taking advantage of her new freedom, she reached over easily to the bedside table. She found the radio. A quick swipe with her freer hand revealed the rest of the tabletop was bare. Then she realized the little cabinet was on castors. Cautiously, she began to maneuver it around with her hand until the drawer handle was facing her. It opened easily. *Oh thank God, it's full of junk. With any luck I might find a hairpin.* The movie escape script was back on track.

The small drawer was stuffed to overflowing, and being blindfolded made it feel like a game as she tried to identify the contents. A knot of silk scarves, no doubt her blindfolds, a container of pills, rubber bands, a bookmark. Then her hand came across cold metal. She withdrew instinctively, recognizing the chilly texture of a handgun even though she had never held one in her life. Holding her breath, she reached out again. Checking she had it by its barrel and not any trigger-happy bits, she gently withdrew it from the drawer.

It was heavier than she imagined a gun should be. Criminals must be really strong. She couldn't imagine waving something this heavy at a bank teller. Gingerly, she set it down beside the radio. What if it suddenly went off and shot her in the head? What on earth was she going to do blindfolded with a gun anyway, except play Russian roulette with doofus out there? And if it came down to it, could she actually shoot doofus if she had to? *Probably.*

Setting the question aside along with the gun, she dipped her hand back into the drawer. This time she found a cylinder shaped thing. She cradled it in her hand, turning it with dexterous fingers. Was it a component of the gun? Was it a silencer? An ammo holder? She felt relieved at the thought the gun might not be loaded after all. Her Braille-like examination found and fumbled a small switch. When she flicked it almost accidentally, the object buzzed into angry action and leapt out of her hand.

She screamed at the top of her lungs. It was an incendiary device! The nut job had guns and explosives tucked away everywhere! Her screaming continued as she vainly tried to lunge from the bed. Her cuffs bruised and grazed her wrists, and the metal headboard shrieked alongside her. The device had rolled under the bed like a hand grenade. For all she knew she only had seconds left on this earth before the timer buzzed and the blast began. Both feet on the floor, her back at an unnatural twist, she almost lifted the bed off the floor in her panic to get away.

Footsteps came thundering down the hallway.

"What the hell!" A quick dive under the bed, and instantly the buzzing stopped. The heaving sobs didn't.

"Hey, hey." She was hushed, as Mickey's warm arms wrapped round her. "Hush now, it's okay. I'm here."

The cuffs were released and she was turned and enfolded in strong arms, her tear-streaked face buried into a soft T-shirt.

"Was it a bomb?" she hiccupped between receding sobs.

"No." Mickey's voice trembled with a suppressed laughter she could feel reverberating in the chest under her cheek. "It was a vibrator."

This did nothing to quell her upset, and a fresh round of crying ensued.

"I...I found a gun, and then that thing just went off in my hand. And you're a lu...lunatic, and you've brought me here and kidnapped m...me." Fat, heavy tears seeped under the drenched blindfold. She was tired of toughing it out, of plotting and planning, and trying to stay one step ahead. Tired of simply surviving this ordeal. So tired of it all. She wanted to go home, to somebody, anybody. She wanted it to be all over. Mental exhaustion made her entire body shake in mild shock.

"Hush, now, hush. You were never in any danger. And you never will be. I promise."

"You had a gun. I found it."

"No, it's just a World War II replica. I'm surprised you could even lift it."

Her tears, hiccups, and a runny nose were mopped up, her back rubbed, and slowly she was maneuvered over to the bed. Her wet, puffy eyes were covered with fresh, cool silk, and she was laid down to be re-cuffed.

"Please don't tie me up. Please. I'm scared. It's cruel, Mickey."

"Hush now. Stop crying. It's all right. There's nothing to be scared of."

"But what if something happens to you?" she wailed inconsolably. "I'll be stuck here and starve to death, and your dog will eat me before my body's found."

"I don't have a dog." Mickey's gentle voice reassured, barely hiding the laugh bubbling under the surface. "I'll hold you till you sleep."

"Flies then, flies will lay eggs in me."

The bed creaked as Mickey lay down behind her and spooned around her.

"Nope, no flies this time of year. Hush now."

Mickey's arm wrapped around her waist, pulling her back into a warm belly and breasts. Long, strong thighs cradled the back of her bare legs. Both were wearing boxers and T-shirts for night attire. It was warm, intimate, and comforting. She relaxed into the human contact she hadn't realized she'd missed during the chilly disintegration of her relationship. Cried out to the point of exhaustion, and soul-weary with the tension of the past two days, she drifted off to sleep on what was no more than an exhaled breath.

❖

The wispy blond hair tickled Mickey's chin, so she moved her head slightly, careful not to wake her bedmate. The subtle movement accidentally grazed Mickey's lips against a pulsing neck. She was so small and defenseless, curled up like a shell. Her skin and hair smelled delicious. The touch raised goose bumps along the arm cradling her sleeping captive.

Mickey listened breathlessly. The touch had not disturbed her. Taking a chance, she reached in again, and placed a deliberate kiss on the same delicate pulse point. She sighed at the rush that ran through her body, and she curved her thighs up tighter, caressing the underside of the legs next to hers. A warm tingle spread through her groin, familiar, although she hadn't felt that way in a long, long time. Mickey cuddled her stolen cargo closer, her hand resting gently on a rising and falling belly.

She frowned as she thought of the scheming deception that had placed this woman in such a vulnerable position. She felt the mysterious pangs of…guilt? Worry? What? She admitted to herself she now felt ill at ease with the whole damned plan. Something lay unsettled in her guts, heavy on her heart, something totally unexpected. She knew exactly what it was. She was hopelessly attracted to the spunky little spitfire wrapped in her arms, and that hadn't been part of the plan.

At first, she decided it was probably eroticization of the power she held over this pretty woman, who fought her every inch of the way. Now she wasn't so sure. Worse than the physical attraction, much worse, was the fact she actually liked her. Liked her a lot. Mickey respected her indomitable spirit and fiery character, her sharp wits and indefatigable intellect. And she hadn't been prepared for that. No, not at all. As with all of their interactions, nothing had been as expected. And now her heart had been overpowered and sneakily ambushed. It was all such a mess. Soon, Mickey knew she would have to let her go.

Eventually, she too drifted off to sleep. Soon a long absent inner peace stole into her dreams and painted them the soft emerald of her captive's eyes.

❖

Deep into the night Mickey's legs entwined with hers, and their mutual body heat became a solder. Clasped in a warm and protective embrace, contentment and the physical stimulation combined into a lethal cocktail. The firm thigh that had crept between her legs became a supple saddle. With a slow undulation, she rode it through her dreamscape.

Mickey responded to the soft grind, pushing her thigh higher into the growing heat. Her lips began a sleepy baby suck, until they found the shoulder of her sleeping companion. As she brushed the skin, the suck turned into an open kiss on the sensitive spot where throat met clavicle. Mickey's eyes fluttered open, but her kiss remained, lips cupping the creamy skin. Her hand drifted up to cup a full breast, the hardened point sitting perfectly in the heart of her palm drawing a throaty, sleep-laden moan from its owner.

❖

Her own moans awoke her. Hands still tied, eyes still blinded by silk, as soft lips trailed up her throat. She was eased onto her back, and she gently opened her mouth to the kiss, to the tender sucking of her lower lip. The hand that cupped her breast began to sensuously circle through thin cotton until she pulsed with every feather touch.

Her lips were stroked by tongue and her breast by fingertips. Slowly, deliberately, the flame inside her was fed. Mickey's body covered hers, increasing their connection between her legs. She opened to accept the pressure upon her center. Their kiss intensified with this primal invitation. A sheen of perspiration coated her body as she moaned into Mickey's mouth, gently pushed her hips up against her. Their tongues touched and rolled and tasted. She was drowning in sensation, drifting on a sea of libidinous need. Her cuffs jangled on the metal headboard, and she broke away to draw in air. To suck up reality.

"No. This is crazy." The words came out dry and hoarse.

"Can't stop. Want this. Want you. Please let me." Mickey's husky whisper slid away into another kiss of caramel sweetness. It pulled her under again, into that swirling sea of need, drinking in lungfuls of this intoxicating torment. Did she want to sink or swim? To drown in these carnal depths by simply handing herself over to her keeper?

"Yes, Mickey. Yes."

Her T-shirt was pushed up, breasts pebbling in the cool air. She arched her back, pouring her flesh onto Mickey's tongue, making her own demands. Now her bonds and blindfold freed her. Without the need to hold on to control, she unconditionally offered up her body.

Long hair brushed across her face and over her breasts and shoulders, before whispering across the fluttering muscles of her belly.

"Oh"—a quiet murmur from below as a flushed face pressed against her stomach. "Beautiful"—another whisper, before kisses were delicately dropped all around her navel. She moaned luxuriously as waves of liquid pleasure washed over her. Her shorts were peeled away and teasing lips traced the fine line of soft down from her navel to her curls. She felt Mickey hesitate, then sensed her inhale her scent. A thick tongue enveloped her clitoris, and all rational thought was lost to the heavens.

Fiery spikes danced along her body as Mickey's tongue explored the length of her sex, in long, luxuriant swirls.

She felt Mickey's finger push through soaked folds and slowly find shelter deep inside. Her hips dictated the rhythm, her moans the music. Once more, Mickey's mouth covered her swollen clitoris, her tongue lying still on its pulse. A second finger pushed hard to load her, to fill her, to stimulate her.

Cupping the exploring fingers, her inner walls melted around them. Exquisite friction built up slowly, rippling through her body, turning her muscles and bones to paste, her blood to opium. She felt it coming, distant, like a brooding storm, then charging toward her faster than her mind could grasp. It was going to engulf her, going to wash her away, break her into little pieces. *I can't do it. I can't let it can't happen. No...No...* But she clung to Mickey tighter than ever. Knowing she would hold her, would see her through.

"Oh, Mickey...oh, Mickey...No...No." She crested, and her cry rang out harsh and ragged in the stillness of the room.

❖

Rising up on her palms, Mickey hovered over her, watching in wonder as she slowly regained her breath.

"Are you okay? Did I hurt you?" Mickey hated that she couldn't see her eyes. She hated so many things about these ties and binds. It would all change. It would all change.

"No. No, you didn't hurt me."

"I'd never hurt you. Never." She lay down beside her, watching her profile, hungry for clues of how their lovemaking had affected her. Wondering if she was as amazed as she was. She became mesmerized by the tilt of her nose rising from under the blindfold, the curve of her cheek, a peach-fuzzed lobe of her small ear. It all distracted and fascinated her, and had from the start, if she were to admit it. And her mouth, that beautiful mouth. She didn't need to see the covered eyes to know the pleasure and sensuality she had given her. The swollen bee-stung pout of her lips told all. She could feel the aftershocks rippling through the stomach beneath her hand. She watched her descend back into her body, back into reality.

In that moment, she wanted to give it all away, wanted to give up everything she had, everything she'd done, live only to please her, to pleasure her, to love her. *To love her? I want to love her. Oh God, how did it all get into such a mess?*

She quickly withdrew from the thought and rose on her knees, gazing in awe at the exhausted but sated body before her.

"Untie me. Please. Please, for just a moment." The voice was small, lost. Mickey uncuffed her.

"Yes, yes, sure. Are you okay?" Her voice was almost a whisper as she pulled the freed wrists into her hands, massaging them. "Can I get you anything?" She held the smaller hands in her own.

"Maybe water, please."

Mickey could hear the stiffness, the awkwardness in the voice, and knew she was struggling with her emotions. She dropped a little kiss on the spent blond head.

"I got bottled water in the fridge. Nice and cold. Give me a minute." Moments passed before she returned, wrestling with a stubborn bottle cap.

"I brought the whole bottle except I can't get the lid to—" The rumpled bed was empty. She froze. "Ginette?"

"I'm not Ginette."

The voice came quietly from behind Mickey. She spun around and had only a shocked instant to register the swing of the replica pistol before it caught her on the temple. She went down like a mudslide. Before consciousness seeped away, plunging her into darkness, somewhere above her the words floated, "I'm Victoria. You grabbed the wrong one, moron."

CHAPTER FIVE

H ey, Michaela? Wake up." A voice was pulling Mickey back into reluctant consciousness. But her head hurt more with every semilucid second. She didn't want to follow the light. She wanted to lie here forever in the murk and never have to exist in the real—and painful—world again.

"Michaela? Michaela?" the voice continued. She tried to ignore it and burrow deeper into the soothing balm of nothingness. *Blissful meditations. Sublime metta bhavana. Free me, for I am lost.*

"Michaela Rapowski. I've got your money for you."

Mickey's eyelids felt as if they'd been stapled to her cheeks, but she managed to painfully peel them open. She moaned as the drumming in her head attuned to each heartbeat. What had happened? Was she hungover? She had sworn never to drink like that again.

"Aha, I thought that might catch your attention." That voice. Her eyes flew open. The voice hovered just outside her field of vision. *Victoria! Shit! What? Hey, I'm tied up?*

"Hello, sleepyhead." The bed squeaked a little as Victoria perched on the edge, helpfully leaning into her line of sight. Squinting through her fog of pain, Mickey looked up into a calm gaze as green as summer meadows. It washed softly over her, and for a hallucinogenic moment, it felt as if the best nurse in the world had come to soothe her, to love her, to take all the pain away.

A small, private smile quirked the corner of the nurse's mouth as she stared down, then a warm hand landed smack, flat on Mickey's belly, causing her to jerk against her binds, setting off another torturous wave of head pain and moans.

"Well, Michaela," Victoria continued cheerfully. "Actually, I think I prefer Mickey, so Mickey it is. Strange how the tables turn. Here we are, you tied to the bed, me up and about. Making decent coffee, using the bathroom unattended, ransacking your hovel of a home." She scoffed at Mickey's wide-eyed alarm. "Oh yes, I've been through all your papers, but apart from confirming you're one Michaela Rapowski, *and* a big fat loser, I can't seem to find what I'm looking for."

Victoria stared at her ex-captor, a thin sheet covering Mickey's nakedness. Victoria quite liked this situation. It was new to her and a little thrilling. She hadn't played kinky games with Ginette, or any other of her few lovers, for that matter. But the concept of power play, in a sexual context, was intriguing to her. With a small shake she brought her thoughts back into focus. She frowned at her mental drift back to last night. Mickey had a strange effect on her that way; she took her mind off to exciting new places. She had to be careful around her. She couldn't afford to lose focus. Especially not now. She tore her eyes away. This would not do, not do at all. She had to concentrate better than this.

She refocused her thoughts. "If you were intelligent enough to ask me what I'm looking for, and let's pretend you are and you have, I'd say I need to know the details of this ransom demand you've made. I need to know the reasons behind it and why it's not been paid. And believe me, these details are the *only* reason your ass isn't on display at the nearest women's penitentiary shower block."

Victoria smiled as Mickey's eyes flashed with anger and more than a little trepidation. Mickey might be keeping silent, but her eyes spoke volumes, and Victoria found herself more than skilled in the translation. *If only I could've seen her eyes instead of being blindfolded. All this would have been over in fifteen minutes flat. I can read her like a crisp new dollar bill.*

Last night, for the first time, she could examine the features of her unconscious captor. Or was it captive? And she had to admit she found the woman attractive. Not in an obvious supermodel way like Ginette, but with a homespun cuteness. Mickey's long, dark blond hair was laced with honeyed highlights from the long summer. Her features gave clues as to her childhood face, a short, straight nose spattered with pale freckles, and a wide, upturned mouth with little laughter creases, and best of all, one errant dimple in the left cheek. In slumber, the little indent was adorable and made Victoria want to dip the tip of her tongue in it. Combined with her big baby blues, Mickey was outright crack candy, and twice as addictive.

Victoria actually had to forbid herself from reaching out to stroke the softly flushed cheek after she had grunted and sweated and manhandled Mickey's lanky frame back onto the bed. And Mickey's body was another landmark discovery. To finally look at it, touch it, after it had been pressed against hers in urgency all night. She was tall, all legs really, but with soft curves and velvety tanned skin. Her breasts were slightly oversized for her rib cage, with small brown nipples. Her hips were curvaceous, with dark curls covering her sex. Slight tan lines showed she sun-worshipped topless but not naked. Three small moles nestled in an arc under her navel. Victoria had traced them gently with a fingertip. They reminded her of Orion's belt. And finally, those big, ugly duckling hands and feet. *Somebody came from farming stock.* Victoria had smiled, running a finger over a ridge of relaxed knuckles before tucking a sheet around the prone body. For the rest of the night she sat quietly contemplating the woman who had split her open like volcanic crust.

This woman was her enemy, she reminded herself over and over again. An enemy who had somehow crept under her skin and under her defenses like a Trojan horse. It confused her, the immediacy of her feelings, the need to be close, to simply sit and watch Mickey sleep. Victoria remembered her touch, and with a blush, each and every detail of last night.

She had to be very, very careful around Mickey. She had skills Victoria had never experienced. Ways and means to emotionally undermine her. To make her want things she blushed to even think about. To make her forget her cold, ruthless life and act like someone she could barely remember. *Thankfully, Mickey, you are blissfully unaware of all this. But believe me, I will do my damnedest to flush you out of my system like the filthy little narcotic you are.*

The only way Victoria knew to negate her emotions was through hard, relentless work, so she turned back to the task at hand. Michaela Rapowski, aka Mickey, and the unpaid ransom. Victoria Gresham was worth millions. Her business empire was worth much, much more. She had been missing for over forty-eight hours. Why then was the world still spinning? How had Ginette missed the ransom e-mails? Where was she? Her ex hadn't moved out of Victoria's home. She should have received these demands.

Why had the police, the FBI, the media, not broken down the door of this shabby little shack and whisked her away in her private jet? The whole situation confounded her. Something was wrong, and she didn't like it. And she intended to get to the root of the problem and resolve it.

"So what say you deal with me, and not the police, and cooperate, hmm? You mentioned something earlier about infringed intellectual copyright. I assume you were referring to yourself and your own…intellect?"

Silence. Victoria sighed. She trailed her fingers across the sheet, up along the flat belly, through that breathtaking valley, up a tanned column of throat, to cup Mickey's stubborn chin. "First of all, I need to know your log-on and password."

"No way," Mickey spluttered. "If you think for one moment—aak." Victoria wrapped a lank of honeyed hair around her fingers and gave a firm pull.

"Log-on."

"Aah. Stop that. You're hurting me. I never hurt you," Mickey squeaked in a wounded voice, on the verge of tears at the sudden hurt.

"Oh, I'm sorry. I never realized there was a code of conduct for kidnappers. Is there a rulebook I need to read? Perhaps it's the *A to Z of Abduction*? No? Then maybe *Kidnapping for Dummies*? But wait, I believe you still have to write that…from your prison cell. The one you'll be sharing with Big Bertha the Bitch Breaker. Tell me the log-on, right now."

"I can't believe you're being so nasty. I was good to you. I could have left you in the garage on that chair, but—"

"Oh, stop the whining. I need that log-on, and I'll extract it like a stubborn tooth. It's as simple as that."

"Well, maybe I'll exchange it for the money you owe me."

"Oh, darling, I'm not in the market, because this information…" She gave another small tug, smiling at the corresponding yelp. *Jeez, I'm not even yanking hard here.* "…I can get for free. So tell me before I get bored and call the police. The only bargaining chip you have is that I want to know what's going on from the inside. So be smart, Mickey, and spill." She finished with another tug to underscore the demand.

"Ow, ow, okay, okay, it's *Victoria*, password *grabber*, with a one instead of the second *i*, and a three instead of an *e*."

"Good girl." *Geez, she has a pain threshold so low an earthworm couldn't limbo under it. What a big baby. I can't believe she crumbled over a little hair pulling.*

Victoria stood over her, the cool air delightfully pebbling Mickey's nipples under the thin cotton sheet. For a split second, Victoria had a flashback to her thunderous, mind-numbing orgasm last night. It was the best sex she'd had in her life. Before, she'd actually believed earth-shattering orgasms only existed in lesbian fiction. Her body blazed, and she blinked hard to clear her head. *No, no, no. The witch is doing it again. For God's sake, concentrate, Victoria. Distance yourself.*

She turned and left the room, returning to the office with this new information. She needed to know what Ginette had or hadn't been up to. Why the ransom demands were being ignored. Something was not adding up.

❖

Mickey ruefully watched Victoria leave. *Oh my God, what a monster! I can't believe she pulled my hair...that's...that's torture. She's a bitch, pure and simple.* She dropped her head onto the pillow. She was flummoxed and worried. This whole crappy, out-of-control escapade had just taken a turn for the absolute worst. How could she rein it back in and turn her luck around? What were her actual chances of survival?

Mickey spent the rest of the morning blindfolded and tied to the bed, listening to a perpetual loop of Swiss cowbells that Victoria had especially downloaded for her.

"It's esoteric." She had smiled cheerfully. "You can meditate."

Drained of all hope, Mickey lay wondering at the type of mind that could so casually conjure up such torment. Victoria Gresham was a grade-A little bastard if ever there was one. A monstrous aberration of Frankensteinian proportions! Despite her musings, she couldn't stop the smile at the memory of last night. Mickey found it hard to equate the small woman passionately trembling in her arms with the little bitch so casually torturing her now.

Mickey knew that last night the tables had been turned on her long before she was clubbed with a replica gun. She'd ambushed herself with the unexpected emotions she'd felt for her prisoner. No matter where she stood, as captor or captive, she couldn't escape her growing attraction for Victoria. The true torture was that Victoria would never see her as anything more than an opportunistic thief.

Sighing heavily through the thirtieth rendition of melodious cowbells, she finally admitted she had been sucker punched. A full roundhouse to the head and the heart. She was seriously attracted to her tormentor. She had dropped her guard, lost her senses, momentarily set aside her plan, and was paying dearly for it now. Victoria Gresham was a witch, an evil, spellbinding sorceress, and Mickey was as witless as a newt around her. The nature of her need alarmed her, dulling her senses and fuzzing her brain. But the real question was how smart would she be when the opportunity came to run? Because it would come and come soon.

The ringing of cowbells was mercifully and abruptly cut off and the blindfold was whipped away. Mickey looked blearily up into Victoria's alarmed face.

"She took it all!" Victoria blurted, eyes wild with disbelief.

"What?"

"She cleared the account. Accounts."

"What?"

"Ginette has cleared all the money out of my bank accounts."

"What?"

"Oh, for God's sake, any more watts and you'd be a lightbulb." Victoria flumped heavily down onto the mattress so that Mickey bounced slightly.

"You're telling me she cleared *all* the money out of your bank accounts when she should have been paying me my *ransom*?"

"Ransom? *Your* ransom? Who's the one chained to the bed, doofus? You know something? I wouldn't leave you in charge of a church collection plate, never mind a ransom note. 'Please, can I have some of your money?' Was that the best you could do?"

"Well, it's not like I write them every day," Mickey shot back. "And I didn't want to sound threatening because I'm not a threatening person."

"You drugged me, you maniac. And tied me up in a cellar. And had a gun. And a bomb. You're telling me that's not threatening?"

"I did *not* drug you. And it was a pretend gun, and anyway, you hit me with it. Hard. And the bomb was a vibrator. And I don't even have a cellar. It was a garage."

"You raped me."

Silence, then, "I never." Mickey's eyes darkened with distress. "I never Gin—Vict—I never. Don't say that," she finished softly, hurt and shame pulsing from her face in waves of scarlet.

Victoria shifted uncomfortably. Her accusation didn't fit well with her either. But she would never admit that to Mickey.

"Well, I was blindfolded and tied up and..." she muttered, feeling suddenly very cheap and dishonest.

Mickey sighed. "How do you know she took your money? Did you check online?"

"No, I sent a carrier pigeon to my bank manager. Of course I checked online. I wanted to know why she was ignoring your pathetic bleats for money. And now I do. The bitch took the opportunity to clean me out while you had me conveniently tucked out of the way."

As Mickey wisely digested this in silence, Victoria continued vehemently, "And the real charm is she'll tell the authorities she took it all to pay the ransom demands *you* so kindly supplied. Not that you'll see a penny of it."

"And she's cleared *all* the money out of your bank accounts?" Mickey seemed stuck in a perpetual loop at Ginette's blatant abuse of kidnapping rules. Victoria glared and waited for Mickey to catch up.

"The bitch." Finally, Mickey managed to break out of her circling pattern with suitable outrage. "We've gotta stop her!"

"And how do we do that, Daisy Duke, when you have us

stuck out here in the rectum of Moonshine County? The money is already gone. Besides, some of the accounts she's plundered… well, I can't exactly go to the police, let's put it that way." Victoria sighed bitterly. "She knows exactly what she's doing, taking advantage of my absence to get away with millions."

"Millions?" Mickey squeaked. "We've got to trace it. She has to put it somewhere traceable. I mean, it sure ain't in the glove compartment of her car!"

"The whole idea is that it *can't* be traced. The accounts she's tampering with belong to intermediary organizations. Shell companies I created to hold my…bonuses."

"You mean offshore laundering accounts." Mickey had her voice back under control. "Somewhere FinCEN can't find it, right?" Victoria winced at the mention of the Financial Crimes Enforcement Network, as if she had heard the most disgusting expletive ever.

Another upset immediately surfaced. Something Mickey had mentioned earlier came back into Victoria's mind with a vengeance. "Hey. What do you mean, you didn't drug me?"

"I mean I didn't drug you. You were drunk on the kitchen floor. That's why I thought you were Ginette."

Victoria frowned. It was true Ginette could be a real boozer when the mood took.

"For your information, I was most definitely drugged. Are you trying to tell me you just happened along, presumed I was my lush of an ex, picked me up, and brought me here? Charming. I suppose that's the only way you can get women into this hovel."

"What do you mean?" Mickey asked hotly.

"I mean I've been looking around while you were snoring. This shack is in the middle of hillbilly country. There's probably not a sane person between here and the nearest fishing hole, gator farm, or trailer park."

"It's picturesque," Mickey said.

"It's Redneck Central is what it is. You sit here all day long, dreaming of big money, playing with your computer…and your vibrator." Mickey's face flamed. Victoria switched straight into business mode now that she had suitably unsettled her adversary.

"Why did you want to kidnap Ginette in the first place? What has any of it to do with intellectual copyright?"

"You stole my idea."

"Your idea? You're a software engineer, so I *stole* your code, right? Did I do this as your employer, or did I climb in through your window one night?"

"Yes. No. I was working for you."

"As your employer, all your ideas concerning *my* business operation are mine. You, as the developer, get credited and handsomely recompensed through our bonus scheme, but the code belongs to the company. It's perfectly legal."

"Well, if I say you stole it then you stole it. I got no compensation or credit. I got fired. You burned me, Victoria Gresham, and I wanted to get my own back."

"A million bucks' worth of compensation? That's what your ransom note asked for. Must have been a really awesome idea for you to deserve that much. What was it?"

"Code FX90."

Victoria stilled. That little bit of programming had proved invaluable and given her company a real edge over their competitors. It ran a calibration that gave out predictive statistics, plus damn good trend factoring and forecasting. All in all, a little honey of a tool, awesome indeed. Still, it never merited a million bucks, not in anybody's money.

"I was never made aware that FX90 was the work of one employee. Who did you submit it to?"

"My supervisor, and then I was told it went straight to your office. They said you loved it and I was gonna get a big fat bonus, then bam! I was out. Turned up one morning and couldn't even get in the door. You conspired against me."

"Look, I have no idea who you are. I'd never even heard of

a Michaela Rapowski until you swooped into my kitchen and snatched me. FX90 was good, but it's just a little in-house tool, likes dozens of others we developed over the years." Victoria spelled it out. "I think *someone* stole your idea, and with it your bonus money, too, and got you kicked out before you knew what was happening. But be assured it wasn't me. I would have kept talent like yours onboard. Did any of your former colleagues know what you were working on?"

"No. Didn't mix much. We were a quiet bunch."

Victoria rolled her eyes. Geeks. "So you have no witnesses. And I bet your machine has been rebuilt. Any other evidence the code's yours?" She picked up her old discarded blindfold and tied it around Mickey's eyes.

"Only on my own home machine. Hey, what's with the blindfold? I already know what you look like."

"You'll see soon enough. Come on. Let's go get lunch." She led her toward the door. Three feet out into the hallway she let go, and Mickey walked straight into a wall.

"Ow. Hey, what did you do that for?"

Victoria sighed. "I could walk the entire floor plan of this place in a blindfold and bump into nothing. You can't even find your own kitchen. Remember that if you ever decide to wander off."

"I've never had to walk around the damn house blindfolded before, now have I?"

"And whose fault is it you're doing it now, hmm? Let's ask ourselves why you are in this predicament, Mickey."

"Is this why you did it? So I'd knock myself stupid if I tried to run?"

"There's no way you'll ever knock yourself smart." She grabbed her arm and redirected her toward the kitchen. "Not even with a ten-pound hammer."

❖

Victoria watched Mickey slowly chew her sandwich. Her face was a mask of concentration and then she suddenly turned to Victoria, a plan obviously fixed in her mind.

"I think I know how to retrieve your money. You're the one who knows where to start. Free me and I'll find your lost funds." She announced her cunning deal. "Bet you one ransom and a head start I can."

Victoria smiled; she had been prepared for this offer. "No ransom. You get your original owed bonus and your freedom. Take it or leave it."

"What? Two hundred and fifty thou? But you're losing millions even as we speak. And here you are trying to bargain me down." Mickey looked insulted.

"This is your chance to break even. You get the money you claim you were always owed, and you get to make things right with me. I think it's pretty damned generous of the universe to give you a second chance. I mean, out of the two of us you're the Little Buddha, Mickey. What do you think? What's it to be, cops or robbers?"

The dry swallow working along Mickey's throat told her she'd hit a nerve. But she also knew Mickey would be calculating the odds of squeezing more out of her.

"I'm not a Buddhist. Meditating to pan pipes doesn't make you a Buddhist." Mickey tried to deflect. Victoria's eyes hardened to flint at the delaying strategy. There was no time to spare.

"In or out? If you can't cope, get off the boat, Mickey." The little dig broke the impasse. It earned Victoria a hot glare and a sullen pout that made the dimple pop. Victoria felt a strange corresponding pop in her heart. *She's doing it again. She's doing that crack candy thing again. She is such a manipulator and she isn't even aware of it.*

"In." Mickey had no other option. It was a fair but totally ruthless offer, considering her alternative was to lie tied to a bed waiting for cowbells to eventually change to police sirens.

❖

A few hours later Mickey had finally pinpointed Ginette's e-signature. It traced across several dubious offshore companies Victoria had highlighted as her own creations, to a bank in Monaco. This particular financial house dealt primarily in currency exchange in a country with extremely high financial caps and soft tax legislation. It was an ideal resting place after the complex network of layering accounts Ginette had been moving the stolen money through.

"My God," Victoria said as she leaned over Mickey's shoulder and glared at the myriad of pages she was pulling up to mark the transfers. "I'd never have believed she had it in her. I knew she was cooking the books, but I never suspected she could manage finance at this level. Boy, was I ever wrong."

"She can't be that dumb. She works for you." Mickey's comment was heavily loaded. She removed her glasses and rubbed her eyes. Victoria shot her a sharp glance.

"How did you know that?"

"I worked for you, too, remember? It was open gossip your lesbian lover was an employee."

"She had a good job in a trusted position, but as we were breaking up she started lining her nest." Victoria grudgingly revealed a personal problem. "Just a few grand here and there out of our private accounts. Nothing corporate." She shrugged awkwardly. "I suppose she was anxious at not managing without me, and by 'me' I mean my money. Ginette always did love the good life. But I never expected this. God, such opportunism. You gotta admire it."

"Well, admire away. There's your money either sitting in or well on its way to Monte Carlo." Mickey casually waved a hand at the screen. "Her entry point was easy since you'd already set up bogus shell companies in several tax havens. You had so many laundering networks it was simple for her to move large amounts of new money through. When it reached the outer edge, it simply dropped off into her own newly created accounts. It's like a game, sort of like Shove Penny at the fairground. Lucky for you, her accounts are all with the same bank. She's basically slowly smurfing all your dollars through your own illegal company accounts, scooping up more and more of your assets on the way."

"Smurfing?"

"Transferring it in small parcels, say several hundred thou at a time, so as not to tip off her host country's financial authorities that something stinks. She's opened several false accounts I can identify, but all the funds aren't there yet. There are still large amounts to be siphoned off from most of your major offshore facilities, but basically, she's sliding through your own laundering services like an oily snake."

Victoria scanned the details Mickey pulled up on the screen. "Yes, you're right. I recognize these. They're my...bonus accounts sitting in my...mmm, hobby companies."

Mickey snorted. "Hobbies."

"Hey. Luxury yachts, fine art, and diamonds happen to be my hobbies, okay? We've all got our interests. You have your computer games. I don't pooh-pooh those."

Another snort. "I don't need to hide my computer games in Belize, or Uzbekistan, or—"

"Oh, quit preaching and help. So how do I stop her from emptying what's left in my accounts? And more importantly, how do I get the money out of her Monegasque accounts and back into mine?"

"You can't. All I can do is show you where it went. It's all under her control now. I mean, you can't really go complaining that your tax evasion funds have been stolen. She's also managed to cover her ass with several of your bogus companies, so if you go sniffing around, you'll blow your own cover. Seems you taught her well, even if it was by osmosis."

Victoria sighed. This seemed as far as she could go for the meantime. The next step required a little more thought and a possible confrontation with her ex-girlfriend somewhere, somehow. Some hope! They sat in contemplative silence until a deep belly growl drew her into the present. Mickey glanced down at Victoria's stomach. She had the grace to blush at its gurgling protests. Mickey looked up. "Time for dinner, it seems. Please let me cook this time."

"Maybe. But you're having a shower first. You stink." Victoria placed a cuff on Mickey's wrist.

"Hey, I thought we had a deal?" Mickey rattled the cuff.

"Yes, and we're halfway through it, and things don't look too good. Last thing I need is you bailing on me, Mickey. You're my Plan B. If things go really wrong, I can always hand you over to the police as my kidnapper and watch my whore of an ex explain where the million for the ransom went. It might be all I recover, but it's better than nothing." Her logic was cold and bitter. Mickey looked at her in dismay as Victoria gently guided her away from the desk. "Did you really think I had no Plan B? Tell me, Mickey, what's yours?"

❖

Victoria sat on the toilet seat filing her nails as Mickey clumsily tried to wash the shampoo out of her hair.

"This is impossible with just one hand."

Victoria scanned Mickey's lean body, water cascading pornographically down its length. *Now I understand why those men's magazines make millions. She's so goddamn goofy and gorgeous, and she has absolutely no idea. Note to self: start porn empire.*

"If I don't rinse out all the shampoo, my hair goes frizzy." Mickey's left wrist had been cuffed to the shower rail above, severely inhibiting her movements.

"So what? Maybe your mother won't recognize your mug shots on the front pages. I mean that's a good thing, right?"

"You know *I* was kind to you. I could have made your past few days miserable, but I didn't, I—"

"Yes, it was peachy," Victoria bit back. "Drugged, kidnapped, and raped. It's all going into my biography, you know. Along with your frizzy mug shot."

"I did not drug you. It was not rape. We were together. We made lo—had sex. It was consensual. Victoria, please don't call it something else." Mickey was anxious and upset now. The cuffs rattled hard against the rail.

"Yes, let's talk about it. Because let me assure you I was most definitely drugged."

Mickey stood silent and stiff as the water continued to stream down her body. Victoria slowly rose and approached, producing a key from her pocket. She looked Mickey square on as she released her hand from the rail.

"You drugged me. And you abducted me. It was premeditated and it was cruel. And yes, we had sex, but I was blindfolded, scared, and alone. You fucked me over on so many levels, Mickey, and for what? Your money? Your dues? Your million bucks? If you'd done your homework, you'd have found two hundred and fifty thousand is the set bonus for the patent of an employee's work, not one million. Two hundred and fifty thousand, *that's* the amount someone else stole from you, along with your precious code. Believe me, I *will* find out who it was, but you'll be incarcerated long before then for this joke of a kidnap. No wonder you're such a loser. You're greedy and you're lazy." She snapped both arms behind Mickey, turned off the water, wrapped Mickey in a huge towel, and then led her back to the bedroom. "Why the hell didn't you turn to me with a complaint instead of rohypnol?"

❖

Now in a big terry robe, Mickey sat tied to the bedroom chair. Victoria hummed tunelessly, as usual, fussing around her as she braided and played with the long, damp hair.

"But I don't want braids! Ow, that hurts. Stop tugging," she said, trying to twist her head away.

"Can it, Heidi. It's braids for you and your rat's nest." Victoria continued working with the hairbrush. "As a little girl I always wanted a Barbie, and you know what Santa brought me? A toy supermarket. So much for lesbian feminist parenting." She wagged her hairbrush in Mickey's face. "But let me tell you, that was the best run play supermarket on my street. All the neighborhood kids dropped in to fill their little toy wheelie carts with the mixed candy I bought for a dollar and sold at thirty percent mark-up!"

Mickey rolled her eyes. It was easy to see where the Business Woman of the Year—several times over—had learned her trade.

"So you're saying if Santa had gotten you a Barbie doll you might be Hairdresser of the Year now? How good would that be? Ow. Be careful."

"Have you got a sensitive scalp or something? I'm barely touching you," she said. "This is great fun. I've always wanted to do this, just never had the right sort of girlfriends."

Mickey almost felt a twinge of pity for her, until her braids were clipped in a pretzel shape to the top of her head. Victoria grinned mischievously. "Oh Princess Leia, you look so cute."

"Enough with the stupid edelweiss hair! You really are one evil little bitch."

Victoria dangled the cuff keys suggestively. "Okay, new Plan B, Mickey. Whether we recover the money or not, you'll go free. But if you help claw most of it back, then that bonus you're owed? Let's call it double or nothing."

"Then you need to give me the security details for *all* the shell accounts you hold." Mickey got down to the real business. "Especially the ones Ginette hasn't gotten to yet. Best bet is to empty whatever's left into a new account we'll set up. At least that money will be safe and she'll have no idea where it is or how to find it."

As she stood to unbraid her hair, Mickey's short terry robe rode up, revealing the curve of her bottom where it met the gentle swell of her hamstrings. Victoria stilled as she drank in the rounded sweep of tanned flesh. Her throat closed, causing her to swallow hard. She was a little surprised at how caught out she felt at such a simple thing as the flash of this woman's thigh. It made her completely lose focus on her plans for life, never mind the next five minutes.

"As for Ginette's new accounts," Mickey said, gathering enthusiasm for her subject, "I can try to hack them, but I'll need as much information as possible. Dates, names, places, phone numbers, lucky numbers. Anything she might use to set up account security for herself." Mickey stopped talking as she realized Victoria was ogling her rather than paying attention. Her eyes darkened and an unsettled look flitted over her face.

Victoria felt her own face flush in an abashed mixture of blatant longing and stinging embarrassment at being caught staring.

"Don't worry. I'm not into sexual molestation," she snapped, surprised at the aggression that crept into her voice.

"I didn't think you were." Mickey came back just as sharp. She was tired of the never-ending implications that last night had not been mutual. That she had forced herself on Victoria, that her kisses and caresses had not been welcomed. It was not her cross to bear that Victoria Gresham had problems processing her own sexual needs and behavior.

"There's still not a lot of money in her new accounts yet," Victoria said, shifting things back to the task at hand. She brought out a bottle of cognac and poured them each a glass. "We need to somehow figure out how to get into them and get my money back out." Victoria was anxious to understand everything about Ginette's actions. "Why is she moving so slowly?"

"I told you. She's smurfing. It's a slow but sure way to sneak money around. Next time you look, you could be cleaned out." Mickey shrugged. "So think about those numbers. I need to break her security. And remember, even though she set up several accounts, the cognitive processes should be recognizable. Once I crack one, the rest will be easier to break."

"God, it's such a unique science."

"Part psychology, part geek, but for the most part, human error. People are lazy when it comes to online security. They don't want to do anything that taxes them too much." She shook her head. "Look at how easy your ex located all your security details the moment your back was turned."

"Oh yes, well, there were dozens and dozens of them," Victoria said. "She had to burrow deep into my laptop to find that index, let me tell you. I still can't believe she managed it. I'm *very* well organized when it comes to money."

I'd love to burrow in your laptop. Mickey's gaze dropped to Victoria's denimed thighs curled up on the seat with her feet tucked under. *God, the cognac's greased my wits. Concentrate on the business at hand. You already know her opinion of you. She's sexually hung up and thinks you molested her, for God's sake. Don't let her catch you looking at her like a moonstruck cow.*

Mickey took another small sip and felt the glow run all the way down to her belly. She sneaked another peek across at Victoria snuggled up in the massive armchair, her blond head haloed with soft lamplight. She felt the warm glow slip a little farther south. The mellow amber swirled in the depths of her glass, Mickey went back to scrying its contents, unaccountably sad that when the purest passion finally entered her life, it was for a woman who thought so little of her. And rightly so.

"Are you sure you can do this?" Victoria looked deep into Mickey's eyes, trying to calculate the odds. But she found their blue intensity behind the glass lenses almost too distracting. "It seems like a long shot. What are the actual chances?"

She pulled her mind back into focus. Her confidence was

wavering. This was the worst run of luck she'd ever endured in her life. Kidnapped, embezzled, powerless...she hated it. It also didn't help that she'd been stupid enough to go gooey over her abductor; to sleep with her, and watch her out of the corner of her eye at every opportunity like some silly schoolgirl. Her cold, clinical life was completely out of balance. She felt she was losing her grip on everything, her mojo, her money, her mind!

"It's up to you." Mickey shrugged. "Even as we speak, your money is hemorrhaging out of your offshore accounts. Our only advantage is we know the depository, and the identity of the accounts she holds in it." She took Victoria's hand in hers. "Look, I have a program that permutates all this information into the most favorable output." She waggled the sheet of paper. "It's worth a try. What have you got to lose, except millions?"

Two hours later, and the permutation program was still running. Mickey glowered at Victoria, who either paced around her small office or sat wriggling on the chair next to hers, poking at her lucky troll doll collection, playing with her pencils, snapping her glasses case open and shut, and generally messing with her neat desktop. Finally, she lost patience.

"Look, go away and make a sandwich or something, would you? You're annoying the hell out of me with all your squirming and sighing."

"Well, how much longer is it going to be?" Victoria snipped back at her.

"As long as it takes. Now go away and stop bugging me. You're ruining my concentration."

"What? The concentration it takes to look at a blank screen? Why can't we have some more music? It breaks the monotony."

"No, you'll only sing along again. Go make some coffee."

❖

The coffee failed to keep Victoria awake. Eventually, the sheer dullness of Mickey's enterprise had her drifting off to sleep in an overstuffed armchair. What seemed like seconds later, a warm hand was gently shaking her shoulder.

"Victoria, Victoria. C'mon, time to wake up."

She snorted herself awake, then paused as she realized she was still free. The tables had not been turned, and she was not attached to some immovable object by cuffs on her wrists. It seemed Mickey and she were indeed in partnership, sharing a new level of trust and understanding.

"Did you know you snore...just a little?"

"I do not." Groggily, she tried to sit upright. "Is it finished? Let me see." She looked up to find her face inches from a bent over Mickey's. Their gazes locked.

"It's cold in here," she murmured, shivering slightly, but not just from the chill.

Mickey swallowed hard but didn't move away. "The other room's warmer." She offered a hand. "Come on."

Heat raced through Victoria's body as their hands touched. No matter the low temperature of the room, it suddenly seemed irrelevant to her body's internal thermometer. Mickey's throat and cheeks turned rose with that flush Victoria knew meant she was responding to her physically. She gave silent thanks to any god listening that she was not cursed with such a telltale sign.

She stood at Mickey's insistence. But Mickey did not step back; instead they stood inches apart. Victoria looked questioningly into Mickey's eyes, and the iris changed from sky to midnight in a blink. Leaning in until their lips barely touched, she closed her eyes and melted into Mickey like heated honey.

Shyly teasing and caressing Victoria gently kissed the coveted lower lip, drawing it into her mouth. With gentle tugs she nuzzled and sucked the sensitive inner silk.

Mickey moaned, her tongue darting out to graze Victoria's top lip, tracing along the bowed curve, exploring form and texture. Bolder, she became more insistent, demanding entry. With one last tender tug to the swollen lower lip, Victoria surrendered and opened to Mickey's questing tongue. It poured into her mouth like caramel, rolling luxuriously over and around her own, numbing her mind to everything except its sweetness.

Victoria was totally lost. She could kiss Mickey like this for hours…for years. If she only knew one thing in this life, it was this kiss. She had always been destined to experience this kiss.

Suddenly, Mickey drew back. "I can't do this, Victoria. Not if tomorrow you're going to say I forced you. I just—" Her voice was broken. "I…I can't. This time you have to want me, too."

Victoria was not bemused and befuddled. She was sure and clear. Her needs stood out starkly before her. All in focus, crisply contoured, sharp-edged black and white, and etched across the open, freckled face looking anxiously down at her.

Victoria had fallen in love, pure and simple. She had lost more than her freedom, more than her money. She had lost her heart to this muddled, deluded, but absolutely maddening woman. *I'm the four hundred and ninety-seventh richest woman in America, and I've fallen for a thieving farm girl in just a few days.* This wasn't part of her strategic planning. It certainly wasn't in her personal mission statement for a rich and ruthlessly successful life.

"Mickey, do as I say," she whispered.

Mickey blinked at her stupidly. Uncertainty clouded her face. "I don't know what you mean. What you want—"

"Mickey, kiss me. It's you I want."

"Oh."

Flushed, Mickey rested her forehead on Victoria's. Eye to eye, they gently smiled at each other before Mickey stole another kiss. *God, how I want her. This small, hard, mean, soft, vulnerable, totally bewitching woman.* This was so out of the box, so unexpected, so unplanned. What the hell was she going to do? Mickey's mind was racing, screaming at her to tell Victoria everything. To confess her sins. *But tonight,* her traitorous heart argued, *tonight add just one more.*

Mickey cradled her in her arms without breaking the kiss. Victoria instinctively wrapped her arms around her as she was carried to the bedroom. Amazed at how warm and protected

Mickey's presence made her feel, despite their short, dramatic history, Victoria realized part of her had always felt secure and cared for around Mickey. Was it this inner security that had finally let her be honest and acknowledge how she really felt? She was thrilled that tonight they would be together again, and this time she would be free to explore Mickey's body. To finally return the offered passion with whispered words and loving touches. Together, wrapped in a hungry kiss, they moved in a daze along the hallway.

"Oh my God. Isn't this just the perfect picture?"

They both swung around.

"Ginette?" Victoria spluttered, shocked beyond belief at the sight of her ex-girlfriend silhouetted in the doorway holding a very non-replica handgun.

Her first jumbled thought was, *Oh my God, she's come to rescue me. How crazy and sweet and...unlike her?*

Then, *What crap timing.*

Then, *I wonder if she's got my money?*

Then, *Wait! None of this makes sense.*

Slowly she slid out of Mickey's arms and onto her feet. All the thoughts jostling for attention in her head went pop as Mickey looked at Ginette and said, "You took your goddamn time."

CHAPTER SIX

Victoria stood frozen, Mickey's nonsensical words ringing in her ears, until a large hand roughly grabbed her by the arm and led her into the kitchen.

"You bastard!" she breathed in utter shock as realization dawned. Struggling in Mickey's viselike grip, she spat, "You're in league with her. The two of you are in this together. You two-faced, underhanded, motherfu—mmph!"

Her angry tirade was cut short as she was roughly gagged. She was then cuffed to the stove handle and pushed down on a seat to fume. Mickey patted the top of her head.

"You're outta this round of negotiations, my little fat cat. Sit nice and quiet. There's a good girl. Ginette and I have a deal to close."

Mickey moved away to switch on the coffeepot, needing to do anything to keep her trembling hands busy. *There's your intervention from the universe. If Ginette hadn't appeared, you'd have blown it all, fallen headlong in love with someone who normally wouldn't even spit at you!* Banging mugs and cupboard doors, Mickey couldn't help but curse the universe and its mysterious ways. But that was the ultimate power of Victoria Gresham. *She so nearly took you for a fool. As if a lady like her would touch you if it weren't in her own interests. You were seconds from giving up your plans, admitting your duplicity, asking her for forgiveness and love, you chump.* She was disgusted with herself for her lies, for her hopes, for being who she was.

Her gaze dropped to the firearm Ginette still sported. "Put the gun down before you blow your foot off."

Ginette delicately placed the weapon on the countertop. She looked glad to be rid of it.

"I've been taking lessons, you know. I joined a shooting club."

"What in hell are you doing coming down here with a gun in the first place?" Mickey frowned, still upset with the intrusion on many, many levels.

"When your e-mails stopped and your cell phone kept going straight to voicemail, I wondered if something had gone wrong. I see something went a *little* bit off plan." She glanced coolly to where Victoria sat with her face scarlet with anger.

Mickey looked over with a nonchalant shrug. "I had to adapt."

Ginette snorted. "That's a new word for it. But I see you survived the frostbite."

Mickey turned to see Ginette gloating over a seething Victoria, who sparked like flint. Mickey was more than glad the little wolverine was chained to the stove. She had a feeling there wouldn't be many recognizable parts of herself or Ginette left if Victoria broke free.

She frowned, not really understanding Ginette's jibe. Victoria was anything but frosty. The woman was full-on lava flow. An iceberg would melt away to nothing just sitting in the room with her, no time for frostbite. She decided the comment spoke more to the breakdown of their personal relationship than the current state of affairs.

"You don't really know her." Ginette glanced over. "She charmed you, Mickey. Another twenty minutes and you'd have forgotten whose side you were on. It's one of her secret weapons."

Mickey felt as if she'd been slapped. It was hardly a lie. Hadn't she been prepared to surrender everything and beg for a fresh start? Was it a Victoria Gresham negotiation trick, or was Ginette upset at what she had seen in the hall? She was the acrimonious ex, after all.

With a steely undertone, Mickey asked, "Where's my money?"

"It's in the car. Just a minute." Smiling smugly, Ginette withdrew to the hallway.

Mickey and Victoria stared at each other. Mickey held Victoria's gaze unflinchingly. Victoria's eyes were luminous with rage, and something else. On a deeper layer, in a secret place, Mickey could almost imagine she saw dismay and abject hurt. When she encountered that, her gaze fell away. She was ashamed.

"Here. Two hundred and fifty grand as agreed." Ginette breezed back in and dumped a gym bag on the table, unzipping the top to expose neatly banded hundred-dollar bills. "You finally get the money she owed you for your work. Good for you, Mickey. It's hard to get her to play fair, but we managed it. Honor even, I do believe. Do you want to count it?"

"Nah." Mickey shifted off the countertop she leaned against and cast a glance into the bag.

Victoria's eyes widened with surprise. Mickey was accepting only the bonus her company would have paid for Mickey's code? Hadn't she offered twice that amount for the partial recovery of her assets? A task apparently just this minute completed? What the hell was going on? Why was Mickey settling for less?

And how come *this* was the ransom amount? The ransom notes she'd seen asked for a million. Ginette had obviously aided and abetted in the kidnapping, but Victoria was beginning to suspect even her ex didn't realize there was a sinister undercurrent to this plan. Dammit, the moment she thought she had a handle on this entire mess it slipped through her fingers.

"What about *my* money?" Ginette demanded warily, now that the deal was actually going down. As if to emphasize her point, she zipped up the bag, shutting the stash away from Mickey's casual gaze. Mickey reached in her pocket and brought out a printed list.

She handed it to Ginette. "These are the details of your new Swiss account. Everything has been moved from the domestic accounts to here." Her tone was flat. "You can check it online. The computer's in the next room."

Ginette glowed with achievement. Waving the list in Victoria's face, she crowed, "See. Every damn thing you thought you could keep from me has gone into *my* new Swiss account. I cleared out our funds, and whiz kid here hid it all away. You'll never touch it. This is *my* alimony and it's going to kick-start *my* new life."

Victoria's perplexed look only encouraged Ginette to explain how clever she was in the greatest detail. "Did you really think I'd settle for your 'good-bye, darling' sweeteners? A nice house? A good job? Oh no, sweetheart, not after I'd been living like a freakin' millionaire for years. I'd fall over and die at my first credit card statement. So our mutual friend here helped me take things into my own hands. I was with you over *two years* and want at least a million for suffering you that long. I mean, seriously, how was a girl like me going to go back to living within her means? Oh no, sweetie, you spoiled me rotten, and there's no way my little Golden Goose was going to get up and waddle off without leaving me a big fat golden nest egg."

Victoria locked eyes with Mickey. A Swiss account? But she'd seen all the money go to Monaco. And the only accounts Ginette could give Mickey details of were their household and savings accounts. *We moved around more money than that, and not to Switzerland. We've been up nearly all night moving every penny I have to Monaco?*

So two hundred and fifty thousand dollars was the price for Mickey to clean her out and set up an account for her ex?

No wonder Ginette had wanted her out of the way. But Victoria still couldn't grasp the full picture. Something was wrong. The simplicity of Ginette's plan hadn't been reflected in the movements she'd seen Mickey make.

Why make Victoria believe it was all a bungled kidnap attempt to grab Ginette? Especially as Victoria was the intended victim all along? Her guts told her Ginette didn't know of this curious little twist. Had Mickey planned to sell her captive on to the highest bidder? But there was no need to try to dupe her into thinking she was the wrong victim to do that. *Dammit, what's she up to? I don't get it.*

The bogus ransom demand was for a million. That was obviously Ginette's alimony claim. And the ransom note would explain to any authorities Victoria wished to inform as to why the money was lifted from her domestic accounts. But why would Mickey settle for a bribe of two hundred and fifty thousand dollars to move the million for Ginette? Because it was all Ginette had to offer?

To Victoria, it was clear that Ginette's pay-off must have been Mickey's original stolen bonus for her code. Her ex had somehow managed to fire, then re-hire, the hapless developer for her own devious ends. It about summed up Ginette as a human being that she'd think that was a sophisticated and clever move. But her bribe amount was peanuts now that Victoria had offered to double it for Mickey's help. So why was Mickey siding with Ginette?

And that help? What actually happened? She'd thought she'd seen *Ginette* emptying her home accounts. Except she now knew it was Mickey's doing with the banking details Ginette had supplied for her. She'd seen the money move with her own eyes, on Mickey's computer. So she'd panicked, thinking it was only the beginning, that Ginette would take more and more. That's when she'd manipulated Mickey to work for her...for her measly bonus and freedom. The irony of her condemnation of Ginette was not lost on her. She was no better.

"And you know what, Vic?" Ginette's crowing interrupted her thought process. "Do you know what the best bit is? You can do nothing about it because the ransom note points to her." Ginette pointed at Mickey, who stood by looking slightly bemused. "That's where your money went if I have to answer to the authorities. So suck that up." Ginette was unaware that she was pointing out the obvious. Victoria had gotten there at least ten minutes ago.

Victoria's eyes locked with Mickey's. *You goddamn fool,* she mentally screamed, hoping the buffoon could read her telepathically, the way some clever dogs do in a crisis. She'd have had better luck with Lassie. Mickey just stared back blankly, like some dumb dogs do. Ginette had set the geek up as the fall guy. *She gets away scot-free, and you'll be forever hunted, and all for your measly bonus? We moved millions around tonight with the details I gave you. What sort of imbecilic crook are you? My reward is far greater than—oh, my God, no!* Her eyes widened in utter shock and disbelief as the penny finally dropped. It was a sting. She had been duped.

"Excuse me, ladies. I hate to interrupt your poignant moment of closure, but I gotta use the john," Mickey said dryly and left the room, leaving the gym bag sitting securely on the table beside Ginette.

CHAPTER SEVEN

G inette moved to sit opposite Victoria.
"I'll take this private moment to gloat. I just love the idea I got one over on the exalted Victoria Gresham. I interviewed her, you know." She nodded to the door Mickey had just exited. "She was a super-geek, a technical analyst for FinCEN."

Victoria's inner alarm bells rang fit to burst her eardrums. Ginette carried on completely unperturbed.

"A little bit odd, but aren't they all? As soon as she came into my office with this brilliant prototype tool—FX something or other—I had her punted off-site quicker than she could blink. It was so easy to set all the blame at your big bad boardroom door. Your rabid shark reputation goes before you in the employee pool."

Ginette smiled endearingly at her. "She was so easy to corrupt. My hard-luck story had you playing the part of my dirty, underhanded ex, and she was on my side from the start. In fact, she even helped me flesh out my kidnap idea. I simply dangled her bonus money like a carrot in front of her nose. It's amazing how easy it is to make people hate you."

She scooted closer and whispered, "I drugged you on your day off. All she had to do was scoop you up off the floor. I told her you have a little drinking problem in case she had scruples about drugs. And then she helped me clear out our joint accounts as well as the household ones. So now I'm free of you and she has the money you 'owed' her for her code. Simple but effective. Everyone's a winner. Oh, well, not you, obviously." Ginette sighed contentedly at her cleverness.

Duh, dumb-ass. Victoria rolled her eyes, looked pointedly at the gym bag, and then at the door. She had to do it several times before Ginette finally frowned.

"What?" she half whined. But it was too late. Already Victoria could hear sirens approaching from maybe half a mile away.

Alarmed, Ginette dashed out into the hall. Victoria could hear her tearing around slamming doors and checking all the rooms before finally rushing back to the kitchen.

"She's gone," she blurted, eyes fixed on the bag. "What the fuck? She ran and didn't even take the money? Do you think she heard the sirens and panicked?"

Victoria raised her chin indicating she had the answer, but she was unfortunately gagged. Hissing with frustration, Ginette scurried behind and none too gently undid the knots. Victoria smacked her lips against the dryness in her mouth.

"She never wanted the money, you idiot. She wanted the security access to my offshore accounts. She's been riding you like the short-assed pony you are. You handed me and our domestic bank details over to her on a platter. All she had to do was make me believe it was *you* emptying my accounts. I should have known you'd never have the smarts to shift money like that. Godammit."

Ginette gawped, the answer not penetrating her brain. Victoria sighed.

"It's over, Ginette. She duped you. She duped us both. Your money is not in Switzerland. It's in Monaco. I saw it there myself, just before I helped her put *my* illegal funds right in there with it. And I bet it's moving out of there even as we speak."

"How did the police find us?" Ginette's IQ seemed to drop in inverse proportion to the rise in siren decibels. She was panicking now.

"Courtesy of our host. This is the smokescreen for her exit. Here we are. I'm chained to a stove, and there's a big bag of money and a gun with *your* prints all over them. I do believe, Ginette, that you look pretty much like a psycho ex who's kidnapped me and cleaned out our joint accounts. Which is exactly what you are. Can you believe that bitch has the nerve to try to bring a moral into the end of all of this?" She gave a bitter laugh.

"What? But you can tell them it's not me," Ginette screeched.

"And confess to money laundering and tax evasion? She's screwed us, Ginette, plain and simple. There's no easy way out of this." Victoria shrugged ruefully. Even the stricken look on Ginette's face did little to placate her. "This police bust buys her all the time she needs to get out of the state. And if she's as smart as I now think she is, out of the country. In fact, most definitely the country. I wonder how long she meditated over this sting."

"You know what really pisses me off?" Ginette spat as she lunged for the gun in her panic. "That you're such a smart-ass about fucking everything. Even your own fucking kidnapping."

"And do you know what pisses me off? That you're so stupid yet I'm the blonde!" Victoria yelled after her as Ginette crashed out of the kitchen.

❖

A smokescreen. A smokescreen for a getaway. *Well, two can play that game*, Ginette's mind screamed as she tore up the hall. She passed the open door to the lounge. *Smokescreen!* The log fire blazed happily. She dashed into the room looking around for anything combustible. Cushions? The rug? She grabbed a throw blanket off the back of the couch, flinging a corner into the fireplace, draping the rest of it out over the floor and up onto the soft furnishings. It smoldered rather than burned. *Damn, pure wool!*

Then she noticed the kerosene lamps decorating each end of an old pine dresser. She shook one. Half full. She hurled it into the fireplace, recoiling at the loud whoosh as it shattered.

The fire exploded out of the hearth, spewing into the room. Rugs, floor planks, couch, anywhere kerosene had splashed, flashed into flame. Black smoke belched up to the ceiling and rolled around the pine beams.

Ginette prayed the distraction of a cabin fire would cloak her getaway down the back roads. She began to double back to the kitchen to grab the money and Victoria. They would pile into her car and run for it.

A muffled boom blew a huge ball of blinding smoke out into the hall. Her vision fell to within a few inches of her stinging eyes. Acrid smoke cut at her lungs. She froze.

Could she plow into the black cloud? Would she make it through or fall, choking after a few steps? Her hesitation wasted precious seconds. The snap and crackle of flames made her stomach shrink with fear. Survival instinct won out. Ginette turned and fled out the front door with Victoria's scream of "What the hell have you done?" ringing in her ears.

She fell into her car and pulled the cell phone from her pocket with shaking hands, hitting the speed dial. A glance in the rearview mirror terrified her. The entire side of the cabin was alive with flame. The roof shingles were engulfed. Smoke plumes and sparks punched the night sky. She stared at the inferno sick with fear. Victoria was still in there, chained to the stove.

The cell phone in her hand spat out a voice, "Ginette?"

She answered as if in a trance. "I set fire to the cabin. Vic's still in there. Oh God. I swear, Mickey, I swear I didn't mean to leave her."

She didn't listen to the answering curses. She knew what she had done.

❖

The smoke was killing her. Victoria could hear the whole house crackling. Wood was popping and exploding. Heated air ran along her skin. And thick, acrid smoke billowed down the hallway, seeping into the small kitchen, slowly asphyxiating her. Her burning eyes poured tears. Her lungs screamed with every sucking breath. She was enveloped in suffocating blackness. She knew she had been abandoned. She knew she was trapped and alone with only her bleak fate for company. *If my life were to flash before my eyes right now, this ending would seem appropriate somehow.*

Glass broke in a windowpane nearby. Glass had been shattering with the heat for several minutes. The same blistering heat was getting closer. Mercifully, it would not be her killer. She would not burn to death. No, she would merely drown in thick smoke.

"Hey! You can't go in there," a man's voice was calling out. "The fire crew's on its way. Hey, you. Wait."

Gunshots rang out deep in the woods. Panicked cries, and then someone was standing beside her. A strong body brushed past her, wheezing, gasping in the acrid gloom. She heard a clank, the screech of metal levered on metal. And then her hands were free, she could pull the cuffs away from the stove. A loud thump as the lever was dumped on the floor. Clumsily, she reached out to her rescuer as a wrenching wail, almost human in its sadness, filled the room around them. A resounding crash, and a scorching wave of heat flooded the small kitchen. Part of the cabin's structure had collapsed, and soon, the rest would disintegrate on top of them.

Strong hands scrabbled for her chained ones. She recognized them as Mickey's. Mickey had come back for her! Into this death trap! They clung together for an instant, both sucking in the clean air that rode on the back of the structural collapse. It was a small reprieve. Flames would find this new fuel, and find them, too. Now their enemy was fire, not smoke. Victoria could already feel heat flaying her skin. The rear of the building was in flames, blocking the exit. They had to move, but there was no way out. Groping through billowing blindness, Victoria lurched forward, dragging Mickey behind her.

Five paces to the door, where the tiles turned to hallway carpet. The heat here was worse, but not unbearable.

Six paces along the hall to the garage door. *Please let the garage still be sound. Please don't let it be a burning wreck.* She inched the door open. There was no rush of heat. It was cooler, with less smoke, but still total darkness.

Fourteen paces now, to cross the floor to the window where the sun had poured in on her first day.

Mickey seemed to sense where Victoria had brought her. She elbowed through the small window, punching out the sharp shards, blood running down her forearm.

Victoria was suddenly lifted bodily and pushed through the opening, until she dropped onto the scorched grass below. She had barely time to draw a cool, clean breath when Mickey landed on top of her.

She lay in a dazed heap, sucking in rasping lungfuls of air when paramedics and police swarmed over her, pulling her clear of the burning building. She was immediately bundled on a gurney and surrounded by the emergency crew. She glanced over anxiously. Mickey had staggered to her feet pushing away helping hands.

"Careful." A gentle hand steadied Victoria's shoulder. "Lie back. Let me fit this mask—"

A shot rang out in the woods. Everyone instinctively ducked. But not Mickey. Victoria saw her standing upright even as everyone dived for cover. A second shot, and more scrabbling from the police and paramedics before it became clear the shooting was too far away to be dangerous.

Victoria lurched upright on the gurney, searching for Mickey through the milling uniforms, blue flashing lights, and swirling smoke. But she had disappeared in a blink, like a magician's assistant.

CHAPTER EIGHT

A nd so, Ms. Gresham…" Detective Spacek continued to report from the foot of her hospital bed. He used the bored drone he'd adopted days ago, when he'd obviously realized his investigation was never going to get anywhere. "After that, we apprehended Ginette Felstrom running around in the woods. She claimed to be disoriented and suffering from amnesia. Forensics showed she had discharged a firearm within the past forty-eight hours, but the weapon has so far not been located. It probably never will be if she just dropped it in the woods during her wandering." His mouth pulled a particularly sour twist, as if he were sucking on something incredibly unpleasant. Victoria coolly observed his discomfort as she sat plumped up on starched white pillows in a private room of the local hospital.

"But we believe it was her gunfire that caused the general confusion among the rescue services, allowing your mystery rescuer access to the burning cabin, and then later, to escape into the woods."

"Ms. Felstrom is a member of a private gun club. It wouldn't be surprising if she had residue from a firearm on her, Detective Spacek." Her voice was still croaky from the smoke inhalation, but improving all the time.

"And your cuffs?"

"A sex game."

He nodded, his withered cheeks not even carrying a blush. He looked pointedly at the dark bruises and cuts still marking her wrists.

They both knew there was nothing for him here. She was the four hundredth and ninety-seventh wealthiest woman in America. She had all the aces and all the answers. And she only played when the odds were in her favor. All that was left for him to do now was to wrap up his report and get the hell out of her hospital room.

"The tall girl that got you out?" Finally, he turned to the last loose thread they both knew would forever dangle, because Victoria was never going to tell him the truth. "You've never seen her before." A statement, not a question. He knew her answer already.

"Didn't see her. Thought she was a firefighter."

He placed his hat back on his head, signaling the interview was over and he was ready to depart.

"Well, I guess I'm done here, Ms. Gresham. I'll file my report. Your lawyers can ask for a copy if you feel the need."

She nodded. "I see. Thank you, Detective Spacek."

Giving a polite nod, he turned to leave, only to bump into Ginette at the door. She had several magazines rolled under one arm and carried two plastic cups of steaming coffee. They eyed each other warily as the detective politely held the door. Sliding past him with not so much as a nod of acknowledgement, Ginette perched herself on the edge of Victoria's bed, scattering the magazines across the covers.

"The vending-machine coffee is atrocious, and it's a good fifteen-minute walk to the local Sludgebucks, so you'll have to make do with this canteen muck. It's pure tar. All you need are some feathers and you got your own revenge kit."

Victoria laid her head back wearily on the pillow, uninterested in magazines and conversation. Ginette prattled on, nodding toward the door Spacek had exited.

"They took so many swabs, prints, and DNA samples, I

could clone myself." She sounded disgusted with the processes of law and order she had been forced to endure. "I mean, I'm innocent, so I should get all that stuff back, right?"

Victoria glared at her, and she shifted awkwardly.

"Well, innocent in that *they* know nothing…that kind of innocent." Ginette tried to appease. Victoria's laser-beam glare remained.

A complete change of subject was in order. *Best turn the spotlight on someone Vic currently despises more than me. I wonder who that could be?* Ginette assessed the situation with Machiavellian shrewdness.

"Did you know the cabin had been rented out in *your* name? Seems that bitch thought of everything."

Victoria's stony silence was fraying Ginette's nerves. She needed her influential ex to be on her side now that all the money was gone. How else was she ever going to recover anything?

"Come on, Vic. She was a bitch, a dirty, two-faced con artist. I was *way* out of my league. I just wanted to stiff you for that big fat bank account and our itty-bitty joint one. Okay, okay, so I'm a bitch, too, but wasn't that one of the things you used to love about me?" She pouted defensively.

She was a very attractive woman and knew it. Her looks and guile had taken her far in life, but under her hardcore materialism ran a mischievous wit and charm that had actually been the glue in her relationship with Victoria. They made each other laugh, they were in synch, and they were real with each other, warts and all.

In fact, if they had never become lovers they would have been firm friends. It was this base foundation of actually *liking* each other in their expensive, shallow, high-maintenance world, where honest feelings never flourished, that held them tentatively together—even now. Especially now, when in the midst of their acrimonious split, they shared a joint problem. They'd both been played for fools. They had both been belittled and beggared by the same scourge. Now they had a common enemy and a common goal. And they knew they worked well together—like the tag team from hell.

"You realize I had to hire practically an entire corporate law firm to broker a deal over my back taxes?" Victoria finally snapped. "The world and his wife noticed the way my money was whizzing around the globe this week. I might as well have stashed it on a roller coaster with fireworks." Victoria shook her head, exasperated. "Of all the stupid, selfish, ill-thought-out schemes. Why did you do it, Ginette?"

"I wanted more than you were offering." Ginette explained as simply as she could. What was the problem here? *You move in with a millionaire and you become used to the luxury. You become addicted to the lifestyle. What's not to understand?*

"I mean, the offer of my own place and a secure job was fine…" Her finger traced an imaginary pattern on the bed cover. "I still have that, right?" She popped a panicked glance at Victoria.

Victoria sighed and merely nodded at her ex's audacity. She just hadn't the energy to scream at her until she turned blue and a nurse with a lot of drugs had to be summoned. So instead she muttered, "Just tell me every stinking little detail…again."

Ginette's shoulders relaxed a little.

"I met her at work. She was another one of those big geeky weirdoes we seem to breed. Anyway, by that time, I was looking for a better settlement. Our arguing had gotten us nowhere, and I knew you were never going to budge. I just wanted some of the surplus money that always seemed to be lying around. Tons of it sitting there all unspent, doing nothing but earning boring old interest." She had a dreamy look on her face as she remembered all those beautiful zeros.

"So you had her fired and withheld the bonus on the code she delivered? Then you used that same money as a bribe for helping you stage a phony kidnapping, so you could strip my accounts."

"Yes. It was a fantastic, uncomplicated little plan. In fact, apart from my withholding her bonus, getting her fired, and blaming you, the rest of it was more or less her idea. All I wanted to do was empty an account or two. She thought up the fake kidnap as a decoy for a huge ransom. It was the perfect cover for the withdrawal of all our funds and meant I could fleece you for even more." Ginette was very frank now that the cards were on the table and at least some of her chips were safe. "All she seemed interested in was her 'honor' and her bonus. Fixated would be the word I'd use. Like I said, she came over as a big geek."

"Except all along she was playing you, turning the plan to her own advantage. You dropped me and all the ammo she needed right into her lap. You said she was ex-FinCEN. She's probably been monitoring me for years, building up her own private profile, planning a move like this."

"If I'd have known you were so crooked, I might have loved you more." Ginette sighed. She was working her way back to Victoria's good side, she could feel it.

"Why on earth did you trust her? How did you know she wouldn't just run for the hills with the money, leaving me locked in a car trunk somewhere?"

"I checked her out. Jeez, I'm not *that* stupid, Vic. The FinCEN information was correct. She's Michaela Rapowski, a technical analyst, and she didn't seem too greedy or creepy or anything. I mean, credit where it's due. She had me running around those woods popping off my pistol so she could drag you out of that furnace. So don't tell me I misjudged the character of the woman I chose to con us out of millions."

Victoria fell silent. She was still struggling to process the behavior of her supposed malefactor. To defraud her, then escape, and then U-turn to save her from a fiery death trap? It told her something. There were clues buried in the actions, motives in the intent, but she was too tired and muddled to connect the dots. And at the moment, it was the least of her worries.

Ginette chattered on. "I mean, I couldn't even tell her I was going to drug you. I had to let on you were a drunk, for God's sake."

"Of course she seemed perfect. She had your number from the start. She was laughing up her sleeve at you all the time, you jackass."

"Well, I don't see why you're so angry with me. *You're* the one who gave her access to everything else."

"I know that." Victoria actually did shout now, only it came out as a strangled rasp. Her throat and lungs were still raw. "She made me think it was a simple kidnap gone wrong. That she was after you. *Then* she made me think you were ripping me off left, right, and center. Made me believe she was helping me hide my money somewhere safe away from your greedy grasp. All the time she was stashing it away for herself." Victoria slapped the bed in frustration. "All along, I thought I was outmaneuvering her. But she had me right where she wanted me, thinking exactly what she wanted me to think. She played me for an absolute fool, with those big blue eyes and dumb-ass dimple."

Aha, at last, the root of the problem, Ginette mused, perched on the edge of the bed. It seemed obvious to her there was more going on for Victoria than just monetary loss. But Ginette needed her to focus on the important things, like lost millions. And her own meager portion of it. This money had to be recouped, and quickly, before the trail went cold. After that, Vic could do whatever she liked with the two-faced scumbag.

"At least I didn't sleep with her," she said casually. It bugged her a little. This was the first salient sign that she and Victoria were truly over and moving on. *And* with that dirty, double-crossing con artist, of all people.

"Oh, shut up."

"We know who she is, we know the starting point is Monaco, and we know we have the resources to find a pin chip in a haystack." Ginette got down to business.

Victoria stared at her, face stern, jaw clenched. It seemed her razor sharp mind was whetted for action. There would be no ridiculous emotions clouding her mind this time, blinding her to cold, hard facts and realistic thinking. Ginette could see the old anger rise in her eyes. *Yes, arise, my beauty. Arise and avenge me!*

"You could have sunk me, Vic, but you didn't. Instead, you were my Get Out of Jail Free card. I owe you, but let's face it, when have I not? And more than anything, I want my money back. She stole from me, too, Vic. Granted, not as much, but it was all I had. Let's go after her. Let's hunt her down and kick that high-up, sexy ass. Let's show her nobody messes with Victoria Gresham and enjoys the dawn."

❖

Two days later, Victoria sat at her poolside table, reading the business pages and sipping a tall vodka and tonic. Her cell phone beeped. She checked the caller ID, then lifted it to her ear. "Ginette…And you're certain…The cash definitely came out of Monaco as sterling…Then back to U.S. dollars. Wow, somebody's trying to cover their trail. Okay, I want you to discreetly make inquiries. My guts say the Caribbean, too. Check out all the currency rates…No, the closer we get, the less I want my name used…Good." The call ended.

She sat and watched the breeze ripple the surface of the pool. Her net was slowly closing in on one Michaela Rapowski, aka Mickey. She smiled to herself. How droll. The casual nickname she had given her was perhaps the only honest thing between them. She had instructed her lackeys to retrieve passport, immigration, family, insurance, educational information, anything they could find on the elusive Mickey Rapowski, though she doubted they'd find much. Ginette was following trails of sterling turned dollar out of the last depository they knew of in Monaco. Somewhere, with a little bit of luck, Mickey would eventually let her guard down and feel safe enough to start spending her ill-gotten gains. Hopefully, they could pick up on it.

Sipping her drink, she allowed herself a small, appreciative smile. The double-cross was perfect, crystalline in its perfection now that she could see right through it. For the hundredth time she played the moves over in her mind.

Victoria now realized that coming out of the Financial Crimes Enforcement Network, Mickey knew exactly who she wanted to target. Probably long before she even joined Victoria's company, she must have been auditing Victoria's darker dealings. Playing on Ginette's greed, she allowed herself to be ripped off, set up as a victim, and inveigled into Ginette's criminal plan. She had actively helped Ginette with the finer points, making it seem like a team effort.

Victoria had smiled grimly at her own little maxim: *There's only ME and MEAT on my team.* Seemed Mickey played the same game.

All Mickey had to do was make Victoria believe she wasn't the intended kidnap victim. Then she could plant a seed that something was going wrong with the ransom payment and let Victoria think she was being double-crossed by Ginette. That part was easy because it was true.

Even when it all went pear shaped and Victoria had overpowered her, Mickey had stayed calm and let the game run on like a roulette wheel. Leaving the ball to drop where it may. It landed well for her. Victoria had picked up on the finances moving around and panicked, as she was supposed to.

Mickey deliberately let Victoria witness the accounts Ginette had given her passes to being emptied, the money crossing the globe along the well-worn illegal routes Victoria knew like the back of her hand.

Her fears about Ginette's sticky fingers were reinforced. All along, Mickey kept her off balance, playing on her fears that her tax evasion hoards were being siphoned off by Ginette. Mickey had worked Victoria's greed in the same way she worked on Ginette's.

Had the seduction also been planned, to keep her distracted, befuddled? Because it had worked like a charm. Spellbinding her even into the present day. Victoria sighed, heart heavy.

Like a fool, she handed over her other account details, and then slept as her funds were casually transferred over hours and borders. Channeled through her own money-laundering routes and offshore companies. When it was done and the money was where she wanted it, Mickey awakened her, and kissed her, and no doubt would have slept with her again, before disappearing for good.

Ginette's surprise arrival had at least saved that little embarrassment. What a strange night it turned out to be. Mickey crashing through a burning building to save her life. Ginette's bumbling appearance saving her heart. Or had it?

Could she ever put a price on what Mickey had really stolen? Could she ever recover any of it? *Run. Run as far and as fast as you can, Mickey. I'm pulling the world apart to find you.*

CHAPTER NINE

M ickey looked across the white stretch of sand to the small oceanfront condominium resort she was now the proud owner of. The azure Caribbean waters of Cayman Brac caressed the bobbing hull of her gleaming thirty-eight-foot sloop. She stood on the oiled teak deck of the *Green Eyed Monster* as she gazed back down into the aquamarine depths. Somewhere down there, if the light was just right and the tide was turning, she swore she could see the same emerald green that made her pulse flutter and her heart leap. She stood transfixed and watched as bittersweet memories washed through her, ebbing and flowing like the warm waters below. Loneliness lapped at her empty hull of a heart, pouring into every chamber. She waited, rolling on idle waves until it came, that soft caressing green, like Victoria's eyes. Taking a deep breath, Mickey pushed off the wood deck and dived in.

Soon she was several hundred yards away from her vessel, farther than originally intended, but she couldn't resist following a small darting school of French grunts along the coral head. Bedazzled by queen angelfish and shy blue chromis, she was happy to follow their lead. It was therapeutic to watch the swirling colors and beautiful marine life of these balmy waters. Over these past few weeks, she had come to know this small bay intimately. From now until midmorning, it belonged to her and her alone, except for the local fishermen who puttered by in their small pirogues on their way to drop nets. It had become her daily custom to dive or swim in the tiny cove in the early morning before returning to her business venture.

Green Eyed Monster had become a regular sight for this small sea-bound community. Mickey whiled away her days sailing and getting better acquainted with the little lady she hoped to spend the remaining years of her life with. Her plan was to disappear for a few years just bumming around the Caribbean and east coast of the Americas on her favorite thirty-eight-foot girl.

A quick glance at her watch indicated her ABT, or "actual bottom time," was closing. She headed back unhurriedly, relaxed and happy at starting another day on this beautiful island. She surfaced and shucked her cylinder and fins onto the broad bottom rung of the stern ladder. She hoisted herself up first, hauling her kit behind her, and was soon safely onboard. She had discarded her mask and regulator before she noticed the set of wet footprints across the teak deck. Frowning at a foot size not her own, she cautiously monitored them as they crossed to the deck hatch and disappeared below.

She remembered the small boat engine she'd heard coming and going earlier. Could someone have taken advantage of her absence to burgle the boat? That would have been unheard of in the local boating community. But still, the damp patches on the deck told their own story. It had to be the electronic equipment that attracted a thief. There was nothing else of value aboard.

Steeling herself for a bunch of ripped out and severed cables, Mickey headed toward the cabin hoping the vandalism wouldn't be too great. She ducked to descend the steps and slowly approached her navigation table. All the equipment looked intact. What was going on here? What did the intruder want? She carried no money or guns onboard, and why weren't there any footprints leaving the cabin?

Her eyes widened in the fraction of a second it took for

the answer to sink in. And in that same second a sharp blow to the back of the head sent her spinning down into the depths of oblivion.

❖

The low thrum of the Perkins diesel and the soft roll of the hull woke Mickey into a world of pain. She tenderly touched her head and groaned. There was a nasty bump, but the skin hadn't broken. It ached like hell. She fumbled for the first aid box and swallowed a couple of strong painkillers.

Motionless, she trained her ears to pick up any clues as to who had knocked her out and apparently hijacked her boat. A quick sweep beneath deck assured her there was no one lurking down here with her. She could hear no footsteps above either, but someone was in control of the vessel. The running engine told her she hadn't been set adrift. But what had her assailant been after?

The electronics were still intact. On closer inspection, they had all been carefully disabled. If she had the right tools, she could have easily reconnected to the outside world and called for help. But of course, the right tools were in a locker in the cockpit. Someone obviously knew what they were doing.

Finally, she moved toward the latched mahogany doors. A gentle push confirmed they were locked from the outside. With her eye to the vent grill, she could just make out a pair of dusky bare feet placed boldly on either side of the ship's wheel. From the size, she guessed that they belonged to a woman and had made the wet tracks she had followed earlier. She also guessed this was her lone assailant. This was the woman who had knocked her out and taken her yacht. But why?

❖

"Can you see anything? What if we've lost her? What if she's running from us? That's not her usual course. Why do you think she's heading north today? Should we follow?" Ginette asked.

"No, I can't see anything, but I can hear something," Victoria replied.

"Oh? What?"

"You," Victoria snapped, lowering her binoculars. "Will you stop yammering in my ear for one second so I can focus?"

Ginette sniffed indignantly from behind the wheel of the rented powerboat. "So you can't multitask? Can't look and listen? Good thing you're only tracking the woman who stole your illicit millions. Heaven forbid you were trying to cross a road."

"Got her. Two clicks north." Victoria was peering intently through the lens again.

"Two clicks? We're in the Caribbean, not 'Nam. What the hell does two clicks mean?"

Without breaking her link with the binoculars, Victoria pointed in the direction she wanted the boat to steer. With a vicious spin on the wheel, Ginette hid a grin as Victoria lost her balance and thumped inelegantly down onto the seat beside her.

Their small powerboat bounced over the waves, intent on following the sleek, white yacht at a discreet distance.

❖

The feet had moved, and no matter how frantically Mickey swiveled her eye, she still couldn't see where the hijacker had gone. She silently cursed her limited field of vision through the vent aperture. All she could see was a few yards of deck at eye level, and then the blue Caribbean sky over the transom.

They had been motoring for hours, and in between bouts of trying to spy and sitting morosely on her bunk, Mickey was beginning to fume. Her shouts had been ignored, whether she chose to threaten or bribe. She still had no idea why any of this was happening. Was it piracy? Stealing her boat for gain, or was Mickey herself the target?

Eventually, the vessel slowed to a stop and the anchor winch rattled out a length of chain. It seemed they had arrived at some sort of destination. A peek through the porthole told her it was the middle of nowhere. Maybe now her questions would be answered. Face pressed against the warm wood of the door, she peered through the small vent looking for clues. Suddenly, a dark brown eye glared right back at her through the tiny opening.

"Boo."

Mickey whipped back, alarmed.

"Gotcha." She heard the deep throaty chuckles, then a growl. "Hey, I'm coming below now, so stand back. I'm armed, and if you even twitch I'll shoot you in the guts without a blink, got it?"

The latch clicked, and Mickey cautiously backed off as the small mahogany doors opened, allowing sunlight to stream into the dark wooden interior. The bulky Glock 33 glinted evilly as she was waved even farther into the recesses of the main cabin.

"That's right now. Hands on your head where I can see them."

The owner of the semiautomatic slowly descended the wooden treads into the cabin. "Turn round. Arms behind you."

The woman darted quickly forward as Mickey complied, and with a double click, cuffed Mickey's wrists together. Mickey was then spun around and pushed down to perch on a bunk.

"Who the hell are you and what—hnghf—" A bandanna appeared, and she was gagged before she could complete her angry question.

Her assailant stood back with a cocky grin. Her grip on the Glock relaxed, letting it hang from her neck on a lanyard, and she folded her arms across her muscular chest. A gleaming smile flashed across a handsome dark face, framed with long, finely twisted dreads, pulled back and tied at her neck with a red cord.

"I'm Bar Jack, and I'm your hostess for today. Now if you'll excuse me, I see we have some company. A little powerboat's been trailing us all morning, so I guess I better go and make them welcome."

With a chuckle, the dark woman turned to leave, clearly satisfied Mickey would not be a nuisance while she dealt with this new threat. As she disappeared above, she called nonchalantly over her shoulder, "Nice to meet you, Ms. Gresham. Welcome aboard."

CHAPTER TEN

For the better part of the day, Victoria and Ginette had attempted to look like sun-seeking tourists, zooming about in their rental powerboat, blending with other pleasure craft. And always just on the periphery of the yacht's heading.

The movements of the white sloop had made no sense, weaving at first in a northerly direction, and then veering off into the shallower waters of a tidal shelf closer to Little Cayman than Cayman Brac. A popular fishing spot, it lay deserted by late afternoon.

This behavior was not the usual routine for Mickey's typical midweek sail, as far as Victoria's privately procured information was concerned. She had paid handsomely for a concise account of Mickey's movements, to be as prepared as possible. Uncertain of her next step, Victoria slowly followed the yacht into the scattered group of reef and rock.

"Have we got the right boat? That's not her at the wheel. In fact, I haven't seen her topside once," Ginette said as she peered through the binoculars.

Victoria cruised to a gentle halt close to a rocky outcrop and roughly propped fishing rods over the side as a rudimentary camouflage for their clandestine activities. It was incredibly difficult to casually stalk someone on the high seas, and she wasn't sure how good a job they'd made of it.

"Let me see," she said as she swapped places. She had been pondering for the past few hours over the irregularity of Mickey's navigation. There was no possible way for the woman to know she had closed in on her here in the Caymans, never mind that Victoria was actually sitting on a small boat spying on her through binoculars. She'd been slowly closing the net on Mickey Rapowski for months, waiting for this very moment. The last thing she needed was to be following the wrong boat.

"No, that's her sloop all right. We even saw her climb aboard as we entered the cove. But I didn't know she had company." Victoria was unhappy with this news. She'd been told Mickey was a loner, a solitary figure never mixing with locals or visitors. On some perverse level, Victoria liked that.

"Maybe it's her girlfriend?" Ginette asked, forever the agent provocateur.

"My source said she didn't have one."

"Maybe she's having a secret affair…"

"No. She's definitely not seeing anyone."

"…and this is where they go for some afternoon delight," Ginette persisted.

"No, it's not her girlfriend. She doesn't have one."

"Maybe they're down below right now, all hot and naked and sweat—"

"It's not her girlfriend," Victoria bellowed, startling nearby seabirds into the air. Ginette innocently reached under her seat and produced the flare gun.

"Why don't you make it a little more obvious that we're sitting behind this rock?"

Victoria glowered as she wobbled back to her passenger seat. Ginette looked at her speculatively, enjoying her baiting game.

"So what now, Captain Softheart? Maybe we should swim over there with knives clenched between our teeth and steal aboard, m'hearty." Ginette rolled her *r*'s and saluted jokily. Victoria whipped around to stare at her.

"What?" Perplexed, Ginette returned her stare, until the penny dropped. "Oh, no. No way. Not me. There's sharks in there."

❖

Much, much later, Victoria really did appreciate the distortion of distance at sea. She felt as if she'd been swimming for a million years. Granted, she was a strong swimmer. A sailing holiday in the warm waters of the Caribbean or off the Pacific Coast was a popular vacation choice for her, but she still felt trepidation as she drew alongside the silent hull. Treading water, one hand on the boarding ladder, she listened for any clues about what was going on onboard.

Her first instinct this morning had been to go back to the harbor, await the return of Mickey Rapowski, then confront her on dry land. However, the unusual activity on the boat and the strange course it had followed alarmed her. She was worried her quarry was fleeing, and her immediate reaction was to follow and hunt her down. Now, after seeing a stranger onboard and no further sign of Mickey, her gut reaction was that something was wrong. But what? And aside from getting her money back, why should she care?

"If it ain't the little mermaid."

She looked up and found herself staring along the barrel of the butchest gun she had ever been on the wrong end of.

"Let's get those little webbed feet up on deck, eh?" the woman holding the gun instructed. Reluctantly, Victoria hoisted herself out of the water.

Slowly, she mounted the boarding ladder and emerged on deck under the watchful and appreciative eyes of the lone gun woman. She was suddenly self-conscious of the scarlet bikini she wore. It now seemed like an extremely stupid idea to swim stealthily out to the yacht to find out what was going on. What was going on was the *last* thing she needed to know. It seemed she wasn't the only one who had a beef with Mickey.

The woman's dark gaze roamed over her body, raising a slight blush to her cheeks.

"So tell me why you been following me around all morning. And just now tried to sneak up on me?" The gun still remained steadily leveled at her while the deep, melodious voice lilted questions.

"Actually, I'm not following you. I'm following the owner of this boat. I have business with her, not you. But finder's keepers, so I'll just jump back in and—"

The dark woman laughed.

"Oh, I can imagine you got business with that one. But there's a waiting list." She turned her head and nodded at the shadowed hatchway to the cabin below. "You have to bide your time to see the elusive Ms. Gresham."

The momentary glance away was all the recovery time Victoria needed to hide her shock. *Ms. Gresham? This woman thought she had Ms. Gresham down below?* What the hell was going on? Why was everything concerning Mickey always so goddamn difficult?

"After you, friend." With a sly smile, the woman with the gun motioned her forward. It seemed she was going to find out.

Doing exactly as indicated by the Glock's muzzle, Victoria climbed down into the cool recesses of the cabin to meet Mickey's startled stare head-on. Victoria's heart lurched. She had forgotten the intensity of that blue gaze. She had seen it in a million shades of sky, and thought of Mickey Rapowski each and every time. And now Mickey was finally before her. Gagged, bound, impotent, and nearly within throttling distance. *And this happens.* From the corner of her eye, she could see the Glock glinting in the dim light from the portholes. *It's so unfair. This woman took everything important from me, and I'm still scrabbling around in her viper's nest of a life.* How hard could it be to get unqualified revenge?

Victoria kept her face passive, giving away nothing of the emotional undertow dragging her under. But she could feel her body betraying her with subtle little tricks she tried to rationalize away.

The tips of her ears heated, but that could have been the beginnings of sunburn. Her vision blurred momentarily, but that could have been the darkened cabin interior. Her stomach lurched nervously, and she felt light-headed, but that could have been the semiautomatic pointing at her. But her heart had no rationale to hide behind. It got straight to the point of the matter. Her heart simply fell in love all over again with the woman perched on the berth before her. With her poker face firmly in place, Victoria ignored Mickey and turned to her armed companion.

"Yes. That's Victoria Gresham, all right. What do you want with her?"

Behind the gag, Mickey was suffocating with an errant heartbeat and hitched breathing. The cabin felt claustrophobic, so crammed with Victoria there was no room for air. Her gaze flicked over Victoria in total confusion, picking up every little hint from her body. Unerringly Mickey read the subtleties. She saw dismay in Victoria's eyes and noticed her flushed face and breathlessness. Mickey drank everything in, every move, nuance, and scent. Every one of her senses jolted and hummed at Victoria's proximity. *Why is she here? Has she arranged this kidnapping?*

❖

Ginette peered through the binoculars until she felt her eyes would bug out permanently. Much to her consternation, she had witnessed Victoria being ordered on board by the sexy black woman with the decidedly unsexy gun. *Shit!*

She knew it had been a wacko idea, but would Victoria listen? No, never. And now it was all dumped on her to be a rescuer, or hero, or something totally alien to her. *Damn it!* So what were the options? Run for help? But in what direction? Ginette looked around the expanse of liquid blue; one wrong turn and she could easily end up in Cuba. Well, a girl could do worse than Cuba, but that wasn't exactly getting her money back. No, she needed Victoria for that, and that bitch Mickey.

Okay, so she had a chart and a compass, but she could never do that "distance times speed, times whatever," formula that Victoria did to tell if there was enough fuel to go anywhere. And she certainly didn't want to run out of fuel out here. Especially not out here.

She could radio for help.

Mayday. Mayday. My ex-girlfriend, the tax evader, has been abducted by an armed hijacker, onboard the boat of an embezzling FinCEN agent gone bad. Please send an honest accountant.

Mmm, maybe not.

The powerboat engine was far too noisy for a sneaky approach. At least not until she knew there'd be a friendly welcome. Perhaps she too should swim out there and do something wonderful to save the day—and her money.

Looking into the topaz blue waters, Ginette shuddered at the hundreds of sharks and giant squid just waiting for her to so much as dip a toe in.

No, better wait and see what happens next. It was late afternoon, and Victoria had only just climbed aboard. At this very minute the skilled and twisted businesswoman was doubtless talking herself out of any tight spot and negotiating a takeover bid.

Stretching, Ginette decided the best course of action she could possibly take was to wait and top up her tan. Who said she couldn't multitask?

❖

"Start by telling me who *you* are." The dark woman leaned back on the galley counter, tapping her fingers absently on the gun that once more hung from the lanyard. Her eyes narrowed to glittering slits.

Victoria answered with the most plausible thing that sprang to mind.

"I'm Michaela Rapowski. I report to FinCEN, and I've been on the trail of this piece of thieving scum for several weeks now."

Mickey's eyes flashed angrily, and a series of anguished squeaks and muffles filtered through the gag. The dark woman processed this information thoughtfully.

"Got ID?"

Victoria indicated her apparel. "Well, usually I roll it up cylindrically and store it up my ass because I'm waterproofed on the inside. But today I just plain forgot."

The woman chuckled. "I can easily check, you know."

"My ID or my ass?" Victoria chanced a cheekily flirtatious route with this charmer. Her gut instinct told her it would deliver better results. Mickey managed to flash a disgusted look from Victoria to her abductor and back.

Another chuckle. "I already checked one. When I reconnect the radio, I'll do the other. Here." Despite the cavalier attitude, she tossed a T-shirt to Victoria. Gratefully, she shrugged it over her meager swimwear.

"Be my guest. I'm with the Boston office," she said, holding out a hand in greeting. "I'm afraid I don't know your name."

"Bar Jack, but they call me BJ." A brilliant smile accompanied her introduction. They shook warmly, hands clasped right in front of Mickey's extremely disgruntled face.

"So tell me, BJ, how come you can check out my ID?"

"I work for FinCEN, too, through an independent agency. We get a lot of your kind of clientele out here in the Caymans. We monitor unusual financial activity and report it to…interested parties. When people like our friend here move onto the Islands, we watch *very* closely. Especially when they make a large cash investment. It draws many eyes." BJ shrugged at the simplicity of it. Mickey blinked worriedly at BJ's answer.

Victoria stiffened slightly. This was the information she needed to hear.

"I audited her trail halfway across Europe, but it faded after sterling changed back into U.S. dollars. The trail was almost stone cold, but luckily, I had people watching the neighborhood down here, too. Always worth a little investigation, a big cash buy like that."

Mickey's eyes widened further, and Victoria gave her a smug look.

"And a police check shows she escaped a cabin fire recently. No doubt a deal gone sour made her run. Why else would she move so fast as to draw unwelcome attention?" A wolfish smile accompanied BJ's words. Mickey's alarmed blue gaze flashed back to Victoria, who now spoke with great care.

"Gresham hasn't been seen publicly since the fire. Officially, she's stood down as director of her corporate interests. Retired early? Gone underground?" She shrugged nonchalantly. "It was only a question of when and where she'd pop up. Scum always floats to the surface." She gave Mickey a long, hard stare, and Mickey glared back with equal animosity.

"It's nice to meet you, BJ. Perhaps between us we can bring this two-faced, double-crossing, underhanded cow to justice."

BJ frowned at the vehemence of the words, and Mickey squeaked indignantly. Victoria gave a charming smile.

"Sorry. I'm very passionate about my work. Big on taxes." Quickly changing the subject, Victoria asked, "So what are the plans for extraditing her? When do we head back to port?"

BJ hesitated. "Mmm, I wasted time today waiting to see what you were up to. I don't know if the boat is rigged for safe night running. The anchor light works, and we're over sand, so I'm gonna sit here tonight and pull anchor early in the morning. You're welcome to stay."

"Sounds like a plan."

"Can I fetch you a drink? That was one long, hard swim," BJ said. It seemed she wanted to keep her unexpected guest close at hand.

CHAPTER ELEVEN

Mickey sat stunned as BJ and Victoria went topside. What an opportunistic, lying little bitch Victoria Gresham was! And what manipulative scheme was she up to now? And what was she doing here if she wasn't behind all this?

In fact, the more Mickey thought about it, the angrier she became. *Little ship's weevil, flouncing round* my *boat wearing that miniscule, indecent...rag. And in front of that ogling, gun-slinging butch. And they're lighting up* my *barbeque. They better not scorch anything...or get grease spots on the brightwork.*

Bare feet padded back down into the cabin. Victoria appeared before her and leaned down to look into her eyes.

"My, it's like looking into a mirror. Hello there, Michaela, or should I say, tricky Vicky?" She smiled brightly, ruffling Mickey's hair. "It's taken a little longer than expected to sniff you out, and unfortunately, it seems the 'friends of FinCEN' have pounced first. Poor Booboo. Of course, the fact they think you're *me* adds an interesting twist, don't you agree?"

Mickey glowered at her, and Victoria's grin broadened.

"Now, I'm not the esoteric one here, so I wouldn't really know. But maybe this little mix-up is the universe telling you you're a bastard for stealing my money and bringing the heat down on me."

Victoria saw no need to inform Mickey that she was brokering a deal with the tax authorities and was practically a legit citizen again. Nor that there was no way the gun-toting butch up top was who she represented herself to be. Let Mickey stew in her own juices for a while. At least until Victoria had figured out an exit from this mess. Mickey glared back at her, the only possible recourse for a bound and gagged woman, as Victoria knew only too well.

"So the way I see it," Victoria continued happily, "is you play along and *be* me, and I, God help me, will be you. We'll ditch Top Gun"—she indicated above to where BJ hummed tunefully over the barbeque—"at the first opportunity, and you'll transfer all your ill-gotten gains back to me. I have the paperwork already prepared and waiting at my hotel room. Then you are free to crawl back to whatever rock you were born under."

Mickey still glared at her.

"Just nod yes, sweetie. Otherwise, you can sit here until BJ's employers figure out who you really are. Then both our asses will be on the line. Except mine will be long gone. I'm not here for you, Mickey. I want the money that you've been throwing around like confetti. It's up to you. But be warned, if you won't play then I'm jumping ship first chance I get, and you're on your own. And I'll bet you my last million dollars BJ's boss doesn't play nice."

Mickey glared at her one last, long time and then nodded curtly. She was busted and she knew it. Best to go with the devil you know at a time like this. And truth was, now that she'd seen Victoria Gresham again, she would quite happily dance after her all the way to the gates of hell. But Victoria didn't need to know that.

"Atta girl, Vicky." Victoria gave her a condescending pat on top of the head, then collected a tray of steaks from the galley fridge before heading back up top without a backward glance.

Mickey sat and fumed. She was playing with a couple of scorpions here. Her instincts told her BJ was way off target as a supposed FinCEN informer, but it might be to Mickey's best advantage to see how things worked out. She had no idea what

Victoria's game was, but it would be interesting to see how she planned to play Michaela Rapowski and get them both out of here.

❖

The smell of barbeque jerked Ginette awake. Sitting up with an abrupt squeak, she examined her slightly pink legs and sighed with relief. She had dreamed she was cooking.

She slapped on another thick layer of lotion and glanced across to the *Green Eyed Monster.* There seemed to be more activity on deck now. She leveled the binoculars at the boat and found the source of the mouthwatering aroma that had hijacked her dream. They were having a barbeque—without her!

We'll soon see about that, she huffed to herself before firing up the engine. *Margaritas, here I come.*

Victoria and BJ looked up at the approaching vessel.

"Ah, I was wondering when your friend would show. See? It took the smell of barbeque to winkle her out," BJ murmured beside her. She seemed pleased at the appearance of Victoria's hidden accomplice.

"Oh. Please. I cracked the cap of the tequila. It's like calling sukie to a pig."

The black powerboat slowed down as it closed in.

"Throw me a line," BJ called out. "Cut your engine and we'll raft up alongside."

BJ's strong arms flexed as she easily hauled the smaller craft in and secured it as Victoria dropped fenders between the two hulls. BJ's movements were efficient and fluid. Victoria could tell she knew her way around a sailing boat.

Ginette stood on the coaming of the smaller vessel to clamber onto the higher hull. BJ scooped under her arms, lifting her easily onboard like a child. On deck, face-to-face with BJ's gleaming smile and wickedly glinting eyes, Ginette stood bedazzled and breathless.

"Why, thank you," she crooned, her fingers still resting on BJ's biceps. "My, but you're strong."

Behind BJ's back, Victoria childishly mimed a gag reflex at the overt flirting. Ginette chose to ignore her. Her quick proprietary scan of BJ's body came to rest on the Glock hanging from her neck and her smile faltered.

"I like your bling," she said dryly, withdrawing. All ideas of flirting quashed. There was obviously a situation going on here, and while Victoria seemed relaxed and not under any threat, Ginette decided she'd better wait and catch the score before investing any further in this interesting stranger.

"Please let me introduce myself. I'm Bar Jack, but call me BJ. And you are?"

Victoria hurriedly took over the introductions, dropping Ginette a few clues.

"BJ, let me introduce you to Ms. Ginette Felstrom. Ginette, BJ is *working* for FinCEN, *too*. She's single-handedly apprehended our target, Victoria Gresham. Who is currently incarcerated below deck."

Ginette drank in these details without batting an eyelash. Inwardly, her mind was spinning. *What the fuck? Why, just for once, can't I appear at a cabin, or on a small boat, collect my money, and leave? Why do Mickey and Victoria have to turn everything into a freaking circus act?*

Victoria continued seamlessly. "Ginette is Ms. Gresham's ex-girlfriend and is assisting FinCEN with its inquiries. This might be a good opportunity for a formal identity confirmation of the woman held below. Ginette, would you like to meet Victoria?"

Oooh, you betcha! Ginette gracefully nodded acquiescence. She had no idea what was going on, but as with everything Victoria did, it seemed Ginette was being dragged along for the ride. Which was only fair, she supposed, considering she'd almost fried her. But she had apologized. Why couldn't Victoria just wrap up this deal, get Ginette back her money, and say adieu?

Why was there always a walk-on role for poor Ginette to ad-lib through?

"Can you tell me exactly what happened, Officer Jack?" Ginette decided to go fishing for herself.

"BJ will do. I'm no officer. We've been monitoring Ms. Gresham for some time now, after an out-of-the-blue purchase of a holiday resort." BJ shrugged. "We think she planned to fake her death in a cabin fire, and then start up fresh in the Caymans. I suppose she thought she could hide down here and put all her tax-free money into legit businesses."

"My, what an absolute bitch."

Victoria looked a little startled at the vehemence in Ginette's voice.

"Spending other people's money like that. Victoria always was born slippy." Ginette continued, warming to her theme. Tucking her arm into the crook of BJ's, she moved toward the cabin hatch.

"She was never good to me, you know." She leaned into the dark dreads conspiratorially. "Very secretive and bossy. And then I was approached by this nice officer...um?" She waved casually in Victoria's direction.

"Rapowski. Officer Rapowski." Victoria sourly filled in the last remaining details for her.

"Rapowski," Ginette repeated. "I'm hopeless with East European names." She giggled up at BJ, her arm now wrapped around a beefy bicep. "When Officer Rapowski here approached me, I could do nothing but offer assistance. After all, I was a victim, too. I had been left alone and penniless, to struggle. No alimony, no nest egg, nothing." She stared up into BJ's bemused eyes. "She lost *all* my savings, you know. In a *very* bad deal."

She delighted in Victoria's bristling at her twist on things. This was the only bit of power Ginette had in this whole debacle. She might as well play it to the max.

"Wow. Now that's bad," BJ murmured in polite sympathy.

"Here, let me help." She gallantly took Ginette's hand as they descended into the cabin where Mickey sat bound and gagged.

❖

Victoria touched Ginette's forearm and looked her in the eye. Here was their easy way out. A simple case of mistaken identity on BJ's part, and all three walked free to get on with the real business of the day—recouping Victoria's money. They could be on that little black powerboat and bouncing all the way back to the hotel in a few minutes if Ginette worked it right. She knew Ginette had the smarts to see it, too. Okay, so they were forcing BJ's hand. She could either keep playing it straight and surrender up Mickey, or she could turn that gun on them. But they had to force BJ to play her hand before whomever she waited for arrived.

As she gazed squarely at Ginette, her mind screamed, *Mickey is the money pot. Let's grab her, load her onto the speedboat, and get the hell out of here.* But she calmly said, "Ms. Felstrom, can you confirm the identity of this individual as Victoria Gresham?" *Come on, G, just say nope, sorry, wrong gal. Never seen her before in my life.*

Ginette looked at Mickey. She broke free from BJ's side and strode over. Towering over Mickey, she spat out, "You bitch." Before delivering a stinging slap to Mickey's cheek.

Mickey sat stunned. BJ looked on in consternation and a tiny bit of amusement.

"I can see you two really did not part on good terms." BJ chuckled.

Victoria blinked in total shock. What the hell was Ginette doing? Didn't she get it? What a wasted opportunity. Damn madwoman would rather bitch slap Mickey than get them out of there. *Shit, shit, shit!* Nevertheless, she grudgingly admired Ginette's take on the spurned ex role.

Mickey's eyes were tearing up, and Victoria shifted

uncomfortably, unsure where Ginette's vengeance trail was going to lead them next.

"Honestly, Victoria," Ginette continued with gleeful malice as she stood proudly over her bound victim. "Did you think I wouldn't find out about your hick girlfriend and your dirty little sex sessions out in the backwoods?"

Victoria and Mickey shot each other stunned looks. Ginette was in full payback mode—for everything.

"I've had it up to here with the two of you, and your loads of cash, and your great sex!" Ginette landed a second slap to Mickey's other cheek. Victoria felt her face flame redder than Mickey's.

"Ahem." Victoria quickly intervened before poor Mickey received another slap for her sins. "All this has no relevance to the case in hand. I think you should stop hitting the accused, Ms. Felstrom." She glared sternly at Ginette, who sighed far too theatrically.

"If I must." She turned once more to a highly bemused BJ, with a half-smile of apology. "I guess I just wanted to get it all off my chest. It's been so painful for me."

BJ extended a hand to escort Ginette back on deck.

"It's not that I'm judgmental. Lord knows, my heart is broken. But Victoria can be such a slut..." Ginette's voice drifted away, along with BJ's comforting murmurs, leaving Mickey and Victoria alone.

With a sigh, Victoria untied the gag and cupped cool hands over Mickey's flaming cheeks.

"Oh God, I had no idea she was going to do that," she said.

"What's her freaking problem?" Mickey sniffled, anger and affront shone in her moist eyes. "Who did she actually think she was slapping? I got confused."

Victoria shrugged. "You, me. Both of us. Who knows with Ginette? Maybe she holds some genuine pique that I had sex with you."

"So what? You *were* exes! She *had* caused your kidnapping.

Why is she even here? Don't tell me you've got back together." Mickey seemed very upset at this possibility, and it showed in her raised voice. Victoria suppressed a smile as she recognized the squeak that marked Mickey's stressed state of mind. Being around Mickey blindfolded for so long had made Victoria very sensitive to her emotional signals.

"Our relationship is well and truly over," she said. "But Ginette *is* invested in this whole mess. In fact, she helped track you to Cayman Brac, and that's why she's here. As for having a go at you…well, let's see. You double-crossed her, ran away with all her money, and it's hard when a relationship ends and the other person moves on quickly. I guess she wanted to hit back at you while she had the chance. And pop a few shots off at me." Victoria flushed slightly as she recalled Ginette's pops. They were a little close to the mark. "She wanted to punish us both, I suppose."

"Both? I didn't see you get bitch slapped."

"Hey. Words hurt, too, you know."

"Well, tell her there are other ways to get closure besides beating up on me," Mickey grumbled on, but seemed more relaxed now that she knew Ginette and Victoria were definitely not an item, and that Victoria had moved on. "You're the one she's really angry with. Why'd I have to get slapped?"

"Again, as Mickey Rapowski you double-crossed her. And now as Victoria Gresham, you're her pain-in-the-ass ex-girlfriend. You're the scapegoat for her current troubles." Victoria shrugged. "Besides, knowing Ginette, I imagine it was plain good fun."

"Can you get her to take the cuffs off?" Mickey nodded up top to where BJ's mellow voice still murmured along with Ginette's soft croon.

"BJ," Victoria called up the stairway. "Throw me the cuff keys. I want to release her, tidy up her face a little."

BJ appeared at the hatchway and glanced down at an un-gagged Mickey, eyes still teared up, cheeks aflame from the slapping. She tossed a small key to Victoria.

"Food's ready. Bring her up when you're done. But remind her I'm still armed and she's still dangerous."

"Let's get you up and out of these." Victoria unlocked the cuffs.

Mickey rotated her cramped shoulders. "So what's next in your great scheme of things? How're we gonna get out of this?"

"Well, Ginette might be just the distraction we need. She's certainly caught BJ's eye." Victoria soothed the flamed cheeks and sweaty brow with a damp towel. "Maybe it can work to our advantage later. I'll think about it more after supper. You know I can't work on an empty stomach." As she cooled the flushed face before her, it took all her willpower not to drop a little mommy kiss on the top of the dark blond head. "There. Good as new. Let's say we go eat and see what else we can find out about our mysterious host."

CHAPTER TWELVE

They all sat somberly at the cockpit table as food was politely passed around.

Sheesh! Mount Rushmore is more animated, Mickey thought dryly to herself, looking at the masked expressions. Everyone had her own secrets to keep, and agenda to slyly impose.

"So, how long were you two together?" BJ swigged her rum, obviously trying to open up a conversation, but managing to scratch open old wounds instead.

"Just over two years."

"Just under two years."

"Forever," Ginette, Victoria and Mickey managed to chorus. Then they sat and glared at each other for the faux pas. BJ looked from one to the other with narrow-eyed suspicion.

"I'm just recalling what Ginette told me earlier," Victoria mumbled into her second cocktail.

"Like I said, just over two years," Ginette snipped icily, glaring at Mickey and Victoria both.

"Felt like forever..." Mickey muttered back, swigging her own rum. "Like being on Death Row." If she had to play Victoria Gresham, then she was damn well going to have some fun with her face-slapping bitch of an ex. "Johnny Cash could have written a platinum hit about it."

A few rums had given her a foolhardy rush of Dutch courage.

Ginette's smoky gray eyes burned holes through her, but damned if Mickey wasn't made of asbestos tonight.

"Only if he sung about low-down, dirty, double-crossing cheats," Ginette bit back. "Oh wait, you are and he did."

BJ and Victoria both shifted uncomfortably at the storm clouds of another domestic squabble on the horizon.

"Anything in his repertoire about lesbian bed death?" Mickey raised an eyebrow eloquently. Victoria's face showed total embarrassment, while BJ took a sudden intense interest in the distant skyline.

"I hope you burn in hell," Ginette spat.

"I goddamn nearly did," Mickey blazed back, referring to Ginette's thoughtless pyrotechnics and Victoria's lucky escape.

"You got what you wanted," Ginette said. "And left behind everything you didn't." Her eyes flicked over to a scarlet Victoria. Mickey's bravado fizzled out into silence.

It was a low blow, but Mickey had hit the nail on the head with the lesbian bed death dig, and it angered Ginette. So she hit back as hard and as low as she could, at the failings in Mickey's own love life. *You chose the money, not the girl, so don't preach to me, you sanctimonious bitch. You hurt Victoria just as much as I did.*

Silence again descended on the small group now that the conflagration seemed to have petered out.

Ginette managed to look peeved and smug simultaneously, and Mickey just glowered. Ginette's comments had stung. The truth was she *had* made a decision; she'd stuck to her original plan and grabbed the money. Chosen the cash over the unexpected emotional connection with Victoria. Mickey knew she had cheated herself, and she had lived with regret ever since. Now the sudden reappearance of the little blond pit bull had churned up all these feelings of doubt and discontentment again. Sure, she had the money and the lifestyle she had always craved, the ultimate irony being it wasn't enough. It felt worthless. Her loot turned into tinsel, cursed by her desire for the very woman she'd stolen it from. Mickey knew that like a fool she had run away with the wrong prize.

Victoria too sat lost in her thoughts, or more accurately her third strong drink. Ginette's accusations had stirred up an anger she had worked so hard to suppress. For the past several weeks, she had put all her energy into tracking Mickey's rapidly cooling trail. At the last minute, her resources had pulled out the connection to the Cayman Brac resort and led her all the way down here. Now that she had her target in her sights, Victoria felt all her old bitterness bubble to the surface.

Her primary motive for hunting down Mickey was to get her money back. But now that she was here, had met her nemesis face-to-face, she was unprepared for the intensity of the hurt she felt. Obviously, she was angry at being kidnapped and the loss of her illicit pension funds. But she was also confused that Mickey had risked life and limb to save her from the burning cabin, only to abandon her again. Victoria was alive today only because of this woman's bravery. Confusion twisted like a knot in her stomach. Distress flooded into her, threatening to spill over as what? Anger, hurt, melancholy, or just plain old brokenheartedness?

There was no doubt that on some level Mickey was as much a hero as she was a scoundrel. But Victoria could have sworn, albeit for one small moment, that there had been some other connection between them. And here, once more in her presence, she felt its sway again.

The sex had been explosive. She had never opened up to someone like that in her entire life. And yes, she could blame it on the kink, on the ties and blindfolds, and the wonderful freedom to just surrender herself to the moment. But never before had she felt so excited, and yet so safe and cared for. And later in the study when they'd kissed? Surely, there had been something more there? Surely, she had not imagined it?

Now her tall rescuer, lover, thief was sitting beside her, so close they could brush arms, raise goose bumps, create static sparks along each other's skin. In a rush of heightened physical response, and clouded, confused thoughts, she felt uncertainty and anger surge through her again. She had been used. Used, betrayed, and abandoned. Mickey had taken everything from her—her money, her passion, her love. It had never been anything special to Mickey, just a way to pass the time in a pokey backwoods cabin.

Was Victoria's life so empty of meaningful emotion that she could surrender her heart so easily to someone who had proven to be the quintessential stranger? She brooded into the bottom of her glass, her own self-disgust fueling her anger.

The ultimate irony for Victoria was that for all intents and purposes, she was now playing the part of Mickey Rapowski. She was the embodiment of her own tormentor.

"Sometimes I just disgust myself," she said to no one in particular. All eyes turned to her.

"I'm such a callous womanizer," she continued bitterly, her voice haggard. Mickey choked on her drink.

BJ watched with concerned curiosity. Never before had she met such a pack of weirdoes as these three. Thank God the one she was interested in seemed the sanest out of the lot.

Ginette raised an eyebrow and waited. Victoria had always been a lousy, introspective drunk. This should be interesting.

"Really, Officer Rapowski? A callous womanizer. How so?" Ginette willingly played devil's advocate to Victoria's alcohol-fueled ramble.

"Oh, I use and abuse. Cut and run," Victoria mumbled bitterly against the rim of her glass.

"Would you say you were emotionally stunted or just a selfish coward?" Ginette offered helpfully.

"Mmm…not stunted. Selfish. Yes. Cowardly and selfish."

"And stupid, don't forget stupid, Michaela." Ginette patted Victoria's arm reassuringly. "Only a cowardly, selfish, dumb-ass would run away from a beautiful, successful, talented woman. After sleeping with her, of course."

"Hey," Mickey hastily intervened. "Maybe…maybe she needed time to think things over. Maybe she never believed she was good enough for a beautiful, successful, talented woman. Ever thought of that?" She raised her eyebrows hopefully as she desperately tried to put her own spin on things. "I mean, commitment's a two-way street."

"Rapowski's heart's on the fast lane to hell," Ginette shot back directly at Mickey. "The officer is obviously a commitment phobe. That's why she can callously fuck over others and simply walk away." Ginette tapped her temple. "Sick in the head but good in bed. And the best women fall for it every time."

"Well," BJ joined in cautiously, unsure of the undercurrents zigzagging through this conversation. "you gotta be careful. Don't want to get your heart slam-dunked."

"Exactly." Mickey desperately embraced a possible ally. "See, the officer's just being cautious. Given a second chance, I bet Rapowski would do the right thing. She's seen the error of her ways. She knows she made a big mistake." She threw Ginette a hard glare. "I bet if she was given a chance she'd turn it all around. Make it better."

"Nope. Once a double-crossing creep, always a double-cross—"

"Yeah, slam dunk," Victoria interrupted harshly, picking up on BJ's metaphor. "But it all depends if you're the player or the ball," she spat out bitterly. BJ and Mickey winced.

Another silence followed as they sipped their drinks. Idly brushing away a wisp of chestnut hair, Ginette finished her third margarita and leaned over to Victoria, drawling seductively, "But I bet you're a bomb in bed, Officer Rapowski."

Victoria's face burned at the memory.

Mickey shifted in discomfort at Ginette's barbed taunt.

BJ scowled.

Way to go, Ginette. Piss everybody off, especially the chick with the big gun! Mickey threw a spiteful glare in Ginette's direction. "That's none of your business. Leave Rapowski alone," she said.

"Actually, I am." Victoria's ears were burning brighter than her cheeks. "A bomb in bed. Sometimes when you're with the right person it can sort of…it can blow your world apart."

Her voice was hard and choked. She was embarrassed for herself, for exposing her anger and vulnerability, for her compulsion to say it out loud and let Mickey know what it had meant to her.

"I…I mean, some women feel special…" She faltered, suddenly deflated. It was as if the words were suddenly impotent now that they existed outside of her. Mickey sat still, her eyes never leaving Victoria's face.

"What a wonderful thing to know. That you made someone feel so special when you loved them," she said softly.

Victoria looked up at her with eyes that were unfathomable. Mickey would have given it all away right there and then to be back in that tiny cabin, holding this small, angry, incredibly hurt woman in her arms, and for once, getting it right.

"I'll take Ms. Gresham below now." Victoria stood, breaking the melancholy that hung over them all. "I'll put her in the forecabin. It has its own en suite. We can lock her up safely for the rest of the night."

"Nuh-uh." BJ shook her head. "I don't want her left alone. Either tie her up or crash in there with her." BJ trusted Victoria Gresham as far as she could chuck a boomerang. There was something about the tall, shady lady that just didn't add up. Truth be told, she wasn't too keen on Rapowski either, but assumed it was some sort of nerdish FinCEN politic because she'd collared Gresham first.

Victoria accepted BJ's ultimatum. With a small nod of her head, she indicated that Mickey precede her down the hatch to her cell for the night.

They moved silently into the small space in the forepeak. Before them, the triangular berth took up nearly the entire cabin space. To the left, a door led to a minute toilet-shower combo, which was in itself a luxury in a boat this age.

Awkwardly, they shuffled around each other, careful not to touch.

"You go first." Victoria pointed to the small bathroom.

Minutes later, Mickey reemerged. "I left you out a spare toothbrush."

"Thank you. And please, no disappearing through the fore hatch. We agreed we're in this together until we can sort out a quick fix, okay?"

"Agreed. Anyway, I don't think I want to sneak up top while Sister Glock is up there with a full glass of rum."

"I meant to ask you about that. Since when do FinCEN's outside agencies go around with the type of hardware that could start an LA gang war?"

"That's just it. They don't."

When Victoria came back, a clean T-shirt and boxer shorts were laid out on the bunk. Mickey sprawled over the top sheet, relaxed and contemplative, looking through the open overhead hatch to the canopy of stars above. Victoria quickly donned her nightwear, then clambered onto the berth and lay down beside her, careful not to touch.

Together they gazed up at the constellations, the tension between them sparkling like the heavens.

"So what is BJ's agenda, do you think?" Victoria asked, hoping to dilute Mickey's effect on her by sticking resolutely to the business in hand. She couldn't fall back into the embarrassing emotional morass she'd wallowed in above deck. Not in a small, intimate space like this. They had to use this limited free time to plan. In a few hours it might well be too late to make good an escape.

"I have no idea, except she's as big a liar as we are. Can't be good for us, whatever her plans are. But as long as she thinks I'm you, then you're safe." Her hand stole across the space between them and gently held Victoria's.

"Still rescuing me?" Victoria smiled bitterly. "I don't need it this time. In fact, I think I'm rescuing you. I think that makes me the hero."

Mickey's response was to caress a thumb across the back of her knuckles. It sent a delicious tingle along Victoria's arm.

"Yeah, but you had to impersonate *me* to do it—oof!" She expelled a puff of air as a backhand landed without warning on her stomach.

"Don't you even try to joke about this, Mickey. Every time you come anywhere near me, something always goes disastrously wrong. All I want is my money and to kick your ass out of my life once and for all. And don't forget it." Victoria tried to sound tough. She needed the distance. Business over emotion every time. It always worked.

"Oh yeah? That's not what that drunken bum Rapowski was saying up top. No, sir. That Rapowski sounded like the kind of woman who would give anything for a second chance to try to make it right. That Rapowski wouldn't run." *That Rapowski wouldn't be afraid to say I love you. To say* I'm so, so sorry, Victoria. Give me a second chance.

"Mickey, that Rapowski doesn't exist."

"She does, Victoria. She so does." Mickey grew deadly serious. It was time to tell Victoria the things she'd spent over two months telling herself. Mickey was lucky to have this last make or break chance.

She took a deep breath. "I'm a fool. I was greedy and stupid. I was everything I'd judged others for. I should have been brave and taken a chance. Instead, I played it safe and stuck to my plan, and I've regretted it every day since. I should have stayed, Victoria. I should have stayed with you. I'm sorry I ran. I'm sorry I cheated and lied." She blurted it all out in a garbled rush. "What can I do to make you understand?"

"Mickey, you robbed me and ran. Like a mugger. What's there to understand? You did exactly what you set out to do. Don't come crying now that I caught you."

"You did *not* catch me. BJ caught me. In fact, she caught *you*. I would not be in this mess but for *you*, Victoria Gresham."

"What? You're in this mess because you stole from me. If anything, this is just desserts. And you're damn lucky BJ got to you first. The way I feel right now, I'd have torn your stupid head off and punted it over the mast."

This was not the reconciliation Mickey had hoped for. The conversation had drifted away from her. She lay thinking how to turn it around, back to where she wanted it to be, where she wanted *them* to be. The air in the cabin grew hot and muggy as the evening breeze dropped away. Turning on her side, Mickey gazed at Victoria's determined profile, the stubborn chin, cute nose, and the sweep of dark brown eyelashes under an arched golden brow. Victoria lay scowling up at the universe. Despite the stern face, or maybe because of it, Mickey took a chance. She blew gently into the fuzzy little ear closest to her, remembering every curve and ridge so well. Then she watched Victoria's face scrunch up.

"Tick tock," she whispered and blew gently again.

Twisting her head around to face her, Victoria demanded, "What the hell are you doing?"

"Tick tock."

"Tick tock what, you imbecile?" Victoria glowered, her face only inches away. "God, I'd forgotten what an utter idiot you can be. How the hell you got away with my money, I'll never know. My wits must have been addled."

"Tick tock. Don't you know I'm a bomb in bed? A time bomb. You've got seconds to defuse me."

Victoria flushed with both anger and embarrassment. "That was just something I said to look like a smart-ass FinCEN agent. I was tipsy."

"Tick tock."

"Oh, shut up."

"Tick..."

"Shut up."

"…tock."

"You're impossible."

"Kiss me."

"No."

"Kiss me."

"No."

"Kiss me and I'll give you all your money back…bar the boat. You can't have *Green Eyed Monster*. I intend on spending the rest of my life with her."

"You're lying to me. In fact, you've always lied to me."

"No, I'm not lying. Every word I say is true. For one kiss you can have all your money back. But I do intend to spend the rest of my life with *Monster*. So make up your mind. Time is running out. Tick—"

"Stop that tick-tocking. It's getting on my nerves."

They lay in silence, face-to-face on the V-shaped bunk under a sprinkle of Caribbean stars. And then without word, warning, or wisdom, Victoria leaned over and placed the sweetest of kisses on Mickey's lips.

Ooh. What have I started? she moaned to herself.

A whimper filled the cabin, deep with need and reverberating with pleasure. Victoria stiffened. *Good God, is that me?* A second ragged gasp assured her, much to her intense pleasure, the whimpers were from Mickey. Comforted by this, she deepened her kiss. She dragged Mickey's lower lip between her own and gently sucked. *Why am I here again? This is the least safe place I could put myself, yet here I am in her arms. These cheating, heartbreaking arms…*

Mickey's hands were running up and down Victoria's back, stroking and caressing through the thin material. Her breathing was erratic, and her heart pounded painfully in her chest. She had dreamed of this incessantly these past weeks, of kissing and running her hands over her golden girl. She felt it so honestly and forcefully she had often woken late at night, confused and sweating in a tangle of sheets. Aching and alone, she would masturbate, and then lie sleepless in emotional turmoil, kicking the covers to the foot of the bed. Thinking of Victoria and that last fraught-filled night. Reliving the choices she had, and regretting the ones she'd made.

And here she was, her Victoria, kissing the strength out of her, turning her limbs to Jell-o, coherent thought to mush, and leaving her wallowing in a quagmire of aching need. Her hands stretched down Victoria's back and cupped her buttocks. Using her considerable strength, Mickey scooped her up to rest on top of her longer frame. She opened her legs to cradle the rounded hips, her calves curved over Victoria's shorter legs to anchor them and pin Victoria down so she could never, ever leave. Mickey was never going to let her go again.

CHAPTER THIRTEEN

G inette traced a casual finger across BJ's cocoa shoulder to her chunky shell necklace. "This is gorgeous. What's it made of?"

"Black coconut and puka shells with a little silver for luck."

"It's beautiful." She withdrew her fingers. BJ smiled, her dark eyes shining in the moonlight.

"Thanks, I made it myself." Her hand came up to touch the trinket. "I'm a silversmith when I'm not sailing the ocean wave." She smiled roguishly.

"Oh? I thought you worked for FinCEN?" Ginette raised an eyebrow, and BJ stiffened.

"I studied silversmithing. What I do to put bread on my table is another thing." Black eyes bored into her. Ginette didn't even blink.

"I think there's more to you than meets the eye, Officer Jack. And I love a mystery."

BJ gave a deep laugh. "I told you, I'm no Officer Jack, and, lady, you wouldn't know where to start with me."

Ginette raised her ring-laden hand and wiggled her pinkie where a heavy silver Claddagh ring with its Irish amethyst heart winked in the pale light. "Ah, BJ, I also wear silver. You never know. I might just get lucky, too."

The breeze dropped, but the temperature held, making it warm and sultry on deck. They sat watching the stars above, finding patterns within the constellations, a diamond, a bullet, a heart. BJ took a long pull on her drink.

"So." She broke the quiet. "Victoria Gresham was your girl, eh?"

Ginette answered warily. "Yes, why do you ask?"

"You don't seem like a match, is all."

"How do you mean?"

"Well, apart from the fact you're angry as hell with her, there's no connection. I mean, you have better rapport with Rapowski than with your ex girl. I guess the breakup must've been bitter?"

"Yes, it was kind of harsh. We hurt each other a lot." Ginette began to twist the Claddagh, head bent, intent on examining each glint as the jeweled heart rotated through the starlight.

BJ watched her silently, sensing the emotional turmoil surging through the pretty woman beside her. Finally, Ginette turned to face her.

"Let's just say the bed death dig was accurate. In fact, the writing had been on the bedroom wall for some time." She sighed deeply. "But after that, much, much later, I did something really stupid and nearly killed her. And when the smoke cleared… literally…I found I'd been lucky. I hadn't lost her. In fact, we both found renewed affection, a residue of our old selves that somehow, by some miracle, mutated into a friendship. A kind of rekindling, if you forgive the pun."

"The cabin fire?"

Ginette merely nodded in answer. BJ read her guilt and shame scrawled across the cast of her shoulders, the tightening of her jaw, and her endless fidgeting with her lucky ring.

"So, why come here with Rapowski looking to arrest her? That doesn't seem so affectionate to me."

Ginette glanced up with a hard smile. "Like you, what *I* do to put bread on my table is another thing, Officer Jack."

❖

The hands squeezing her bottom were burning an imprint onto her flesh. Her hips were rolling over Mickey's center like tide on sand. She couldn't stop it if she wanted to. *How the hell did I get into this? Why am I here sucking on her neck, trying to kiss every inch of her? God, I'm an absolute junkie for her. I've no control. I'm so lost in all of this.*

Mickey pushed her hips to answer Victoria's rhythm. She couldn't believe Victoria's heated fervor. Victoria had never been the aggressor in their short-lived liaison. She had always been the pursued. Mickey was the initiator. At least that's how she'd imagined it. Where had this hotheaded hellion come from? In all her fantasies she had been the one chasing…and losing, reliving her miserable mistake over and over. The object of those fantasies had sprung into her arms, and was now pinning her to the bed, forcefully taking her. All she could do was hang on, and she fully intended to do that.

Victoria's hips stilled their grinding motion, her lips stopped sucking Mickey's throat, and she pulled away. Leaning on her elbows, she gazed directly into the lust-hazed face below. The rebalance of weight pushed her mons harder onto Mickey, who gave a small grunt and sneakily spread herself wider, trying to apply some of the pressure to just the right spot. Feeling the furtive move, Victoria eased her weight off, using her knees as leverage. Amused, she watched Mickey's small, petulant frown at this loss of contact, then she snapped with sudden authority, "Put your hands above your head."

Mickey's frown remained, and her hands stubbornly squeezed Victoria's bottom. The soles of her feet continued caressing Victoria's smooth calves. Her dimple popped as her lips pursed.

Oh no, you don't. Don't you dare turn that damned dimple on me. I'm on to your tricks, Rapowski. And I'm in charge now.

"Do it," Victoria ordered.

Mickey eased her grip and placed her arms above her head. Victoria raised herself to straddle Mickey's prone body, unceremoniously stripping Mickey's boxers down, leaving them at a constricting half-mast, pinning the tanned thighs together. Never breaking eye contact, she caught the rim of Mickey's T-shirt and yanked it off, exposing full, mouthwatering breasts. Toffeed nipples puckered for her invitingly.

"Close your eyes, and don't open them."

Mickey complied immediately. Victoria stripped away her own nightwear before repositioning herself across the captured thighs. She sat there and contemplated the body beneath her, her musk and heat dampening Mickey's darker curls. It was the complete reverse of their first time together. She didn't know why she needed this tokenism, other than to feel that this time she was in charge, the bestower of exquisite touches and delicious kisses.

She watched the hitch in Mickey's breathing and the rise and fall of her chest. She smiled at the struggle Mickey was obviously having keeping her eyes closed and her hands above her head. It was a delightful little power game. Already, she could see Mickey's eyelids fluttering as she was torn between the wish to obey and the need to look at Victoria straddling her nude. The earthy scent of moist arousal rose up between them. The tension crackled like a fuse.

Mickey whimpered, and Victoria pulled a nipple deep into her mouth before her teeth closed around its base. Mickey arched up into her mouth gasping at the stinging caress. A soft tongue bathed the ache away in long, swirling strokes. Artfully, it dragged across the sensitive bud as recompense for the tingling ache, before it began all over again. Her other breast was cupped and kneaded firmly, fingers pulling on the pouting tip before circling and compressing the soft tissue. This pattern of flattening, kneading, and pinching continued until Mickey's breasts hummed with sensation. Each alternately massaged and stroked, as its twin was sucked and laved by Victoria's hot, greedy mouth. Mickey arched, pushing onto Victoria's hands and lips. She squirmed and groaned, the pressure between her trapped thighs building to the bursting point.

"Please, Victoria," she whispered. "Don't torture me."

Victoria sat upright and undulated her sex across crisp curls. Mickey gasped, her hips surged trying to make a connection for her pulsing clitoris, but her thighs were restricted, pinned torturously together.

Victoria was determined to increase the torture. She reached for Mickey's twitching hands, lying on the pillow on either side of her head, and clamped them onto her own breasts.

Mickey's eyes flew open. Automatically, her fingers began to greedily knead the beautiful creamy flesh spilling onto her cupped palms. She massaged lustily, pale pink nipples peek-a-booed between her fingers, teasing her until she ached to kiss and bite and suck them. They were both groaning now. Victoria held Mickey's hands in place as she ground her hips and rode out her pleasure.

Eyes wide open, greedy hands full, Mickey decided the rules were broken and the game was now officially over. Thus justified, she rolled Victoria onto her back and rested snugly between her open thighs. Quickly kicking off the offending boxers, she grunted as she arranged her outer lips, at last making sliding contact with Victoria's engorged clitoris. Leaning forward, she captured her lover's gasping mouth, only releasing their bruised lips to draw breath.

She sensed Victoria approaching orgasm, and she reached down between their hips and steadily pushed two fingers deep inside her. She swirled them on the long, slow slide in, stroking the inner walls all the way along, giving a sensation of complete fullness. Satisfied by the small grunts and puffs that told her Victoria was comfortably filled, she began to stroke in and out. Victoria cried and arched into her hand. She opened wider to give Mickey more access, feet planted firmly on the thin mattress for leverage.

Mickey's thumb grazed across her clitoris causing another throaty cry. Mickey watched the passion ripple across her face. On and on her fingers slid, each thrust greeted with a deeply delicious moan.

"I've dreamt of you every night," she murmured in a pink-tinged ear, her thumb stroking softly across the swollen clitoris. "Stay with me," she whispered her secret need.

Victoria did not register her words; she was floating in her own world. She gave up trying to kiss, or hold, or stroke the woman above her, and simply surrendered to the rippling waves of orgasm that washed over her again and again, pulling one long, ragged cry of ecstasy from her screaming lungs.

"You're so beautiful," Mickey whispered as she watched Victoria crest.

❖

BJ's and Ginette's heads jerked simultaneously. The animal cry of raw release roared out from the open fore hatch and ripped the night apart. BJ looked at Ginette in shocked alarm, as if misunderstanding what she was hearing.

Oh, way to go, you horny sluts! Ginette thought, disgusted. *Blow our cover completely, and leave me up here with the angry gunslinger to try to explain.* She turned to BJ with her best full-on smile.

"My. Now there's a whole new slant to coming onboard."

CHAPTER FOURTEEN

"You two! Up here now." BJ bellowed through the cabin hatch. "All three of you got some explaining to do." She'd had it with these stooges.

Grimly, she sat beside a silent and very tense Ginette, her hand resting on her Glock. A few minutes later, two flushed, incredibly shamefaced women seated themselves opposite. Ginette threw a hard, unforgiving look at both of them, taking in the rumpled sleepwear and guilty faces. Victoria looked everywhere to avoid Ginette's stare, while Mickey became fixated on her own feet.

"Spill." BJ folded her arms, commanding everyone's attention. "Who the hell are you people? What the hell's going on here?"

Mickey and Ginette both turned silently toward Victoria.

"Great. It's always up to me to sort everything out." She flung her hands up in disgust. The other two rolled their eyes at each other.

"If you're gonna wear the general's stripes, you gotta run the war," said Ginette.

"First"—Victoria jabbed a finger in BJ's direction—"get rid of the hardware. I'm *not* telling you anything as long as that gun's lassoed around your neck."

BJ gave her a measured look. She quickly surmised there

was no denying the request, not if she wanted answers from this stubborn, shady trio. Slowly, she slipped the semiautomatic from her neck, setting it carefully on the seat beside her. She sat back and waited.

Victoria took a deep breath and began to explain in one huge rush. "*I* am Victoria Gresham and I came to Cayman Brac on the trail of Michaela Rapowski, who stole all my…private funds, with the aid of my ex-girlfriend Ginette Felstrom, who nearly killed me in a cabin fire that Michaela Rapowski subsequently rescued me from before disappearing to…well, Cayman Brac." She finally took a breath. "And there you have it. Right cast, wrong script."

BJ blinked. "You're not Officer Rapowski?"

"Nobody's Officer Rapowski," Mickey said. "I was never a federal agent. I worked for the Financial Crime Enforcement Network as an analyst but left over a year ago. I helped with an unresolved investigation into businesswoman Victoria Gresham's supposed laundered assets. I then used that information to set up a sting. And I used Ginette Felstrom, Victoria's ex, to gain an entry point."

"Sweet," BJ said dryly. "So tell me who you are, not who you ain't."

"Mickey Rapowski, kidnapper, swindler, and thief."

BJ next turned to Ginette. "And who are you?"

"Oh, I'm Ginette Felstrom all right, and I'm a victim of these two, just like you. I was dumped by her"—she pointed at Victoria—"and double-crossed by her." She singled out Mickey. "And now I have to be nice to *everyone* in order to get my life savings back." She managed to sound simultaneously flirtatious yet outraged at the injustice heaped upon her.

BJ shook her head slowly. "So between the lot of you, I got a tax embezzler, a kidnapper, and an arsonist, at the very least. My, how'd I get so high up in the world? If my mama could see me now—"

"And what about you, *Officer* Jack?" Ginette interrupted. "What have *we* got with you?"

BJ grinned. "You got a pirate."

"Oh, perfect." Victoria slapped her hands on her knees. "Absolutely perfect. We've got Blackbeard onboard. And just what does a pirate want with Victoria Gresham?"

"And where's the rest of your gang?" Mickey threw a furtive look around the horizon. "Pirates don't work solo."

"The rest of the crew are arriving later this morning, after I fix the radio and call in our position."

"But what do pirates want with Victoria?" Ginette repeated Victoria's question.

BJ shrugged. "A ransom. All them millions she's got stashed away."

"What millions?" shrieked Victoria, pointing at Mickey. "She's got all my millions. Kidnap Rapowski. Leave me out of it."

"Well, we thought she was you." BJ frowned, still a little lost in the maze of twisted identities.

"*We?*" Ginette asked.

"My uncle Rudy, he's the boss." BJ came clean, caught up in the need to try to make all this mud as clear as possible.

"Rudy? As in my hotel manager Rudy? Scumball. Setting me up like that. Selling me out." Mickey was beside herself with outrage. "I pay his freaking wages."

"Hey." BJ frowned. "He's the only scumball in my family to hold down a nine-to-five."

Victoria swapped glances with Ginette. "He's also our informant. Rudy's the guy who sold Ginette all the details of your movements before we came down here."

"Told ya. Scumball," Mickey said.

"I was making inquiries all over the place trying to trace her." Ginette pointed accusingly at Mickey. "He must have figured his new boss was the tax evader Victoria Gresham using an alias.

Half the underworld knew FinCEN were after her when her money went whizzing round the globe so openly." She shrugged away the bad luck of it. "Rudy did good research. A little bit off center, but kudos."

They all looked at her as if she was insane.

"Hey, credit where credit's due," she said. "After all, the man found a link between Rapowski and Gresham. And then sold it to us. That's good work. Okay, so he jumped the wait list and tried to kidnap her for his own gain. But I got nothing against the guy for going after her." She jabbed a finger in Mickey's direction.

"Except he thinks I'm her." Mickey nodded toward Victoria, scowling at Ginette's stupidity.

"Is there anybody involved who isn't a double-crosser?" Victoria asked in exasperation. Silence followed.

She sighed. Negotiations were going to be tricky.

"So what happens tomorrow morning?" she asked BJ. "How does all this work?"

BJ frowned. "I don't really know much because I'm sort of lowly, like a cabin boy sort of thing. In fact, I only got dealt in because I'm family and trying to pay off my student loan. But as I understand it, she"—BJ pointed at Mickey—"has been kidnapped by me. And a ransom demand has been made to Uncle Rudy, by himself."

Mickey sighed as she guessed the rest. "Which he'll pay immediately—to himself. In a brown paper bag, I bet, without contacting the police as per the ransom demand." It all sounded so familiar. She should have patented the formula.

"As we speak, he's happily emptying your office safe and business accounts. But he wants more than the immediate cash, he wants the rest of your dirty money, and he knows it's stashed away somewhere semilegit."

"And then what happens?" said Victoria. Everyone was being very free and easy with her money here.

"Mmm." BJ looked rather contrite. "I think he comes out here, tortures you for the rest, then kills you."

This was greeted with absolute silence.

"Oh," Mickey said. "Kudos. Credit where credit's due," she quoted, glaring mockingly at Ginette.

"I wonder which one of you he'll torture first," Ginette said, looking innocently from Victoria to Mickey.

With a lingering, spite-filled glare in Ginette's direction, Mickey turned to Victoria, slightly panicked.

"If there's gonna be any torture, let me still be you, okay?" she said.

"Ha," Victoria guffawed. "What happens if he pulls your hair? You'll spill like a kicked bucket."

"Okay, fine. So we're *all* gonna die." Mickey flung her hands in the air. "We're shark fodder."

The words had an almost magical effect on Ginette. "Shark fodder, my shiny white ass," she screeched.

Leaping to her feet, she grabbed the Glock and took a stance on the cabin roof, where she glared defiantly down into the cockpit at her companions. They all froze.

Victoria was the first to speak. "Careful, Ginette, point it in the air, in the air."

"Yeah," said BJ with an anxious frown. "It's a hair trigger, and the safety catch is—"

"Don't tell me what to do with a gun," Ginette seethed. She was sick and tired of all this danger, and drama, and no money. "You forget I've had private lessons at an *exclusive* Boston gun club. I know *exactly* what to do with a firearm like this." And she hurled the thing overboard.

BJ's jaw dropped faster than the gun on its way to Davy Jones's locker.

"My gun. My beautiful Glock. It was a Christmas present from my brother."

"Way to go, Ginette. Now we can keep the bad guys at bay

with bad language and rude hand gestures," yelled Mickey, giving an example of the latter.

Victoria turned immediately to BJ, who stood transfixed watching the ripples spiral away from her Glock's watery grave.

"Okay, BJ, the tide has turned. You're either with us or against us. Are you onboard, or do you follow the gun?" she asked coolly while BJ stood stunned, blinking at the water, obviously in turmoil.

Victoria plowed on, knowing her quarry was off balance. "What was your cut for the kidnap and extortion? Oh, and let's not forget my grisly murder."

Without waiting for an answer, she immediately began to sweeten the deal while BJ was still reeling. "Because I can guarantee I can better it."

BJ turned dazed eyes to Victoria. "I was to get the boat," she said.

"The boat?" Victoria and Mickey asked in unison.

"Yeah, *Green Eyed Monster*. Rudy was gonna give her to me for minding you overnight. She was to be 'sold' to me just after her owner's unfortunate disappearance overboard. Seemed like good pay at the time. I mean, she's a beauty. And I *was* to be off sight for the actual murder part." BJ sounded eerily sincere. "That way it would hold no bad memories for me."

"*My boat*?" Mickey howled in anger. Totally overlooking the murder and memories part. "No way. Absolutely. No. Fucking. Way."

"Actually, she's *my* boat," said Victoria. "My money bought her, so in effect, I own her."

"Okay," Mickey huffed. "You can get tortured on her, then."

"About that." Ginette joined them in the cockpit now that she had successfully disarmed the wrong team. "Why don't we just pile into the powerboat and run away? Cuba is over there." She pointed to a distant horizon.

"I'm staying and fighting for *my…my* goddamn boat."

"If Rudy finds you all escaped, I'll be sleeping with my Glock."

"Cuba is in the opposite direction, you ditz."

"Hey! I'm only trying to be helpful," Ginette snapped back at the chorus of put-downs.

"Helpful. You just threw our only freaking weapon overboard. It's a pity none of us are on insulin, you could toss that, too," Mickey yelled.

"Stop being such a sarcastic twat," Ginette hissed.

"Maybe if I had a crutch you could bend it around the mast."

"Mickey, you're hysterical. Stop it now." Victoria spoke sharply.

"I'll get you a crutch, all right," Ginette muttered under her breath.

"Ginette, I heard that. Either you two shut up or I'll lock you both down below," Victoria said before sitting down, head in hands. "Quiet, all of you. I need to think this through."

She turned to BJ. "An old tub like this is pretty poor payback for aiding and abetting in a kidnap and murder."

"Hey. She's not an old tub. She's a 1958 classic sloo—"

"Shut it, Mickey." Attention back on BJ, Victoria continued, "I'll give you half a million…when I get my money back, that is."

"Half a million?" BJ blinked at her with astonishment. "To do what?"

"Whatever I say, of course."

CHAPTER FIFTEEN

Victoria and BJ faced off. The night sky was fading away as a new day dawned. Decisions had to be made; lines had to be drawn.

"And her," BJ said and indicated Ginette, "I want her." Bravado had returned tenfold to her voice and mannerisms. After the shock of her Glock's unceremonious burial at sea, BJ was now compensating for the temporary loss of her machismo. The slightest flicker of hesitation passed through Victoria.

"Done."

She and BJ shook hands.

"What?" Ginette squeaked, while Mickey just snorted derisively.

"You owe me one very expensive Glock. Not to mention its sentimental value." BJ scowled at her. "This needs to be settled."

"You're getting half a million bucks. Go out and buy a gun shop," Ginette shrieked.

"It's a matter of honor. I would not be a pirate if I let you just disarm me like that without retribution. I got a code to keep."

"What code? You're a silversmith doing a favor for her uncle. This is fucking ridiculous. Victoria, I need a word." Ginette pulled Victoria to one side and whispered heatedly, "Since when did I become your chattel?"

"Oh I don't know, since you tried to abduct me, fry me, embezzle me, double-cross me, throw our only gun overboard, slap people—"

"Will you stop listing every little thing? Have you never heard of letting go?" Ginette sighed. "Okay, so I'm a shit. But I'm *not* yours to be brokered in a deal as some sexual plaything." She sneaked an appraising peek over at BJ, who was patiently waiting for the outcome of this tête-à-tête. "At least, not for any longer than a week."

Taking advantage of their one-on-one, Victoria reached for Ginette's forearm. "I know what we need to do," she murmured quietly. "I have a plan, but one of us will have to set it up. I can't tell Mickey, at least not yet. I'm still unsure how much of BJ's loyalty I've bought. So that leaves you and me, Ginette." She looked deep into the eyes of her former partner, wondering how strong their newfound friendship actually was. "I need to know you're in this with me, right to the end."

Ginette looked back at her, her gaze serious and unswerving. "But this is the end, Vic. Sink or swim. There's nowhere else for us to go, now is there?"

"So, what's the plan?" Mickey's soft gaze turned to Victoria. It was filled with hope, expectation, and something unquantifiable that caused a jolt of raw emotion to slam through Victoria's body. *My God, we're hours away from becoming plankton, and with one look she has my knees turning to pudding. I've got to keep her away from me, at least until this is all over.*

Victoria took a deep breath as her pulse rate finally settled. "I need you to go to the bow of the boat and just stand there."

"Okay." Mickey stood to obey unquestioningly. "Why am I doing that?"

"You're keeping a lookout for pirates!"

"I'm on it." Mickey made toward the bow with determined purpose. Victoria blew out a long puff of relief before BJ's quizzical gaze caught her eye.

"Ain't no pirates here until I give out our position."

"I don't want her to know the plan just yet."

"And what plan is that?" BJ asked.

"That we may have to sink *Green Eyed Monster*."

"Oh, please, can I be the one to tell her?" Ginette asked, delighted.

"Ginette, if Mickey finds out, you know she'll not go along with it and we'll all end up feeding the fish. What means more to you, pissing her off or saving your shiny white ass, as you so eloquently put it?"

Ginette sat down and silently sulked. Victoria turned to BJ and continued, "We need a safe port, a fast PC, and a lot of luck. What can you deliver?"

"Port and PC."

"Let's get going. Rudy will be wondering why you haven't reported in by now. They'll start searching the area soon."

BJ nodded, releasing the lines that lashed the powerboat to the side of the yacht and then securing the smaller vessel astern for towing. Next, she started up the engine and shouted forward, "Raise the hook, Mickey."

She looked across the wind-whipped deck to Victoria. "We're heading for Little Cayman. The wind's behind us, and we'll make good time. I live near Grape Tree Bay. We can moor offshore."

"What about a computer?" Victoria stood beside BJ as the wooden hull began to cut water.

"Use mine. Can't think what else to do. Home will be the last place Rudy will look." At that, the cell phone on her hip vibrated. She unclipped it and read the caller ID, then casually hurled it in a high arc into the passing waves.

"The search is on." Her fingers tightened on the wheel.

"That damn boat's slowing us down." Mickey grimaced at the small speedboat bouncing and yawling behind them on its short towline. "Cut her loose."

"No, we'll need it later," Victoria protested.

"Then I'm hoisting the main to get some extra speed."

Mickey unwound the halyard on the main and began to haul canvas.

"There's something on the horizon," Ginette called from her lookout.

"Where? Is it Little Cayman?" Victoria asked anxiously, trying to ascertain where Ginette was actually looking.

"No. If that were the case, I'd say there's an *island* on the horizon. What I mean is there's *something* on the horizon. That's what I say when I don't want to alarm everybody by saying there's bloodthirsty pirates off the port quarter."

Mickey grabbed the binoculars from her and looked. Shrugging, she handed them over to BJ. "Don't recognize them, do you?"

BJ raised the glasses. "Yeah. We got bloodthirsty pirates off the port quarter."

"Let's try to haul the powerboat alongside. I know we're moving, but we have to do this before they're close enough to notice or care that we have an auxiliary vessel," Mickey said.

BJ wrapped the line around a winch for more purchase, and with her and Mickey's muscle power, they managed to drag the bouncing craft alongside starboard.

"Victoria, jump in and start her up. Be careful, hon. Aim to land on the seats."

Uncertain of where this was going, Victoria made the leap onto the awkwardly bouncing smaller craft and immediately fired up the outboard.

Mickey nodded at Ginette. "You next. Hurry." But Ginette pulled back, hesitating and looking over to Victoria in question.

Before Mickey could rush Ginette along, BJ interrupted her. "No. You go. It's Victoria they're looking for, and they think you're her. They'll torture you both till they find the real one. You two know where the money's at and how to get to it. Ginette and I are useless to them, and as Rudy is my uncle, I might have a little sway yet."

"As long as it's not from the yardarm." Mickey gave a grim smile.

"It's the best odds we got." BJ shrugged. "Stay to starboard. Hide behind us as long as possible. The later they see you, the better your chances."

Mickey nodded grimly and jumped several feet to tumble in beside Victoria, tilting dangerously until a hand reached out to steady her.

"Here, catch." Ginette passed Mickey's diving gear over the rail into waiting arms. "Take it, just in case." She reached down and untied the final line connecting the two craft and tossed it into the black speedboat. Ginette stood by the guardrail looking down at Victoria. They exchanged one long look that held their good-byes.

❖

"Will Rudy be with the pirates?" Ginette asked as she watched the powerful motor cruiser slowly gain on them. Even at full sail, full throttle, and with a strong lead, it was only a matter of time before the faster craft caught up.

Shielded from the oncoming vessel's view, Victoria and Mickey had gradually peeled away, merging into a small fishing flotilla that had fortunately crossed their course. It was easy for the two white women to look like nosy tourists on a day's outing.

"No," BJ snorted, keeping an eye on the pirates' heading. "He gets seasick. He's safely tucked behind a desk counting his grams and dollars."

"Grams? He runs drugs, too?"

BJ shrugged. "Small time. This motor cruiser gaining on us is one of his ponies. The Gresham money was to put him in with the big boys."

"Do you do any drug running for him, BJ?"

BJ's answer was to spit into the wind. "No damn way. Keep

that shit away from me. I even hate I had to grab the Gresham lady. But I owe Rudy my college fees. My debt was big." She bit her lower lip then looked directly at Ginette. "I made a mistake. I see it now. I'm sorry I got your friend in danger, and I promise to do all I can to help change things."

Sighing, Ginette turned seaward. Their pursuers were even closer. It seemed they were gaining at every passing second. It was nearly time to put Victoria's plan into action, and she could feel fear clawing at her belly already, making her limbs heavy and her head woozy. *I don't think I'll ever be brave enough for this life. All I seem to do is hover around the periphery of courage and success, hanging on to better people like some gawping onlooker.* "And I'm sorry about your gun," she said.

"Best thing you could have done for me. No weapon, no target, as they say." BJ smiled at her and caught the seed of fear buried in Ginette's eyes. "Don't worry. I'll never let them hurt you."

"That's not going to happen, babe." Ginette smiled back as bravely as she could, understanding BJ's intention. She moved forward and dropped a soft kiss on BJ's lips. "Let's see what we can do to even the odds a little. Are you a gambler, BJ? Because I am." As she spoke she opened a locker and pulled out several of Mickey's emergency fuel cans, stringing a long line through the handles and tying them at regular intervals.

"What the hell you doing, girl?"

"Party prepping. I like to mix things up a little." She attached one end of her line to the bow, the other to a cleat at the stern, and gently lowered the whole string of fuel cans to just above the water line on the starboard side, away from the view of the oncoming vessel. "Can we head for shallower waters?"

BJ nodded. Sailing on toward Little Cayman was bringing them into a series of shallows. She changed course slightly to accommodate whatever crazy scheme Ginette had going on.

Ginette noted that the faster motor cruiser changed direction and followed, slowly closing in. And behind it scooted a little black powerboat, the kind rented by holiday makers. With Victoria in a scarlet bikini and Mickey in a cut-off wetsuit, they looked like vacationers out for a day of fun.

Ginette watched the echo-sounder as the depth fell away beneath them.

"Let's drop sail now and motor slowly onto that sand bank."

"You want to run aground?" BJ looked dismayed. Ginette watched the motor cruiser close in. They had maybe ten minutes if they were lucky.

"Aye, Skipper, I do. We're out of time, out of sea room, and out of luck. Let's jam her here." Despite the lightness of delivery, her steady gaze was crystal clear and deadly serious. "At least this way they only get to cart us away. They'll have to leave *Monster* behind. And maybe Vic and Mickey can reclaim her."

BJ shrugged and watched mystified as Ginette took the longest halyard that ran all the way from the masthead and tied it discreetly to the port grab rail. Ginette had a definite plan. Her last movements had been as precise as they were confusing.

"Remember to keep them port side of us," Ginette said as BJ spun the wheel and brought *Green Eyed Monster* to a shuddering halt, the deep keel driving hard into the soft sands underneath.

BJ cut the engine and waited to be boarded. Carefully, Ginette readjusted the line of plastic fuel cans just below the starboard waterline. She had loosened a few caps, and small traces of gas seeped out in rainbows on the water. With a wild wave toward the circling black powerboat, she turned back in time to see the pirate vessel arrive on the port side.

Ping! Out of time.

❖

"Having some trouble, Bar Jack?" a voice crowed from the motor cruiser as it slid alongside. "Lost your bearings and run aground?"

"Morning, Carmelo. Why are you hounding me today?" BJ flung back casually, her arm draped over the wheel as three of the visitors leapt onboard. She hated this guy, Rudy's nastiest, and luckily, his densest henchman. Carmelo advanced with a leer, leaving his crew to tie up alongside.

"I'm hounding you because you're one two-faced bitch." His smile suddenly turned cold. "And Rudy's gonna gut you when I drag your sorry ass back. Family or no."

He next turned to Ginette. "You must be the fancy fuck I gotta cut the fingers off till you remember all your account details. Rudy says to tell you he's missing his pretty lady boss."

Ginette gave a sickly smile at the idiot's mistake. Another one who didn't know who the hell he was chasing. What was it about Victoria? It wasn't as if she had a forgettable face. How perverse she should finally cop for her ex's torture. *Ah well, proof karma really does suck.* Leveling her best millionairess sneer at the second rate henchman she drawled, "Well, if you cut of my fingers, how can I write you a check?"

"On board now." He thumbed over his shoulder to his boat and waiting men, "Both of you. God, this piece of crap stinks of fuel. You musta ruptured a fuel line, asshole." He pushed BJ hard ahead of him and grabbed Ginette tightly by her upper arm.

"Think you're clever running aground, BJ? Think these flash vacation fuckers gonna come running over to help? That they might take you off this tub and somewhere safe?" He smiled. "Hard luck, these cunts don't give a damn. They're too busy enjoying themselves to even look at you."

"Well, that lady over there is waving," Ginette said pointing at the little black powerboat that could easily dart across the sandbar with its shallow hull. She waved back. "Oh look, she's even going to summon help. How kind of her."

Carmelo squinted in surprise at the vessel she was pointing at. His eyes widened at Victoria in her red bikini waving back at them. They widened even more as he saw her lift the flare gun.

And they nearly fell out of his head as she pointed it, not at the sky, but straight at the wooden hull of the *Green Eyed Monster*.

"Fuck! Everyone off, everyone off. Now!"

But it was too late. The flare popped and shot forward in a crazed stream of smoke, hitting the fuel-soaked hull point-blank. With a crackling roar, flames erupted, glazing across the white hull in a swirling liquid dance. Even the sea alongside leapt with a short-lived wave of fire as billowing red smoke enveloped everything. As each semisubmerged fuel canister ignited in turn, small booms and flashes rode up into the air through a festival of red flare smoke. It was a display that got the attention of every living thing in that sector—man, fish, or fowl.

There was no way an incident like this would go unnoticed and unreported. It was clear that Carmelo had to get away before the authorities came looking. He leveled his gun at BJ for a clean shot before he ran, only to find empty swirling smoke. Cursing, he latched on to Ginette's wrist, dragging her to his vessel, where the crew were desperately trying to get free of the burning sloop. Ginette knew it was the last thing any sailor wanted, fire at sea, but to be actually attached to a burning vessel was tantamount to suicide. They had to get away, and fast.

Ginette resisted as much as she could, but not so much as to get a split lip, and allowed herself to be manhandled aboard. As they passed the port grab rail, she un-slipped the halyard knot she had tied earlier. Keeping a tight hold on the length of line, she led it onto the motor cruiser. Her sleight of hand went unnoticed in the pandemonium.

Carmelo roughly shoved her down on the deck. "Sit, bitch, and shut up. One twitch and I swear I'll blow your fucking ugly head off," he barked before running to the pilot's deck to scream at his helmsman. Ginette smiled quietly as she quickly looped the sloop's halyard hard to a stern cleat of the motor cruiser, tying both vessels together.

Let's see you outrun Monster now. Dusting her hands with a satisfied grin, sharks or no, Ginette calmly stood up and jumped overboard into a smoke-red sea.

❖

"Here, give me your hand. Give me your hand." Victoria reached out for BJ and hauled her closer to the powerboat. With a grunt, BJ gained leverage and easily pulled herself up and over with minimal effort.

"That bitch of a girlfriend of yours kicked me overboard. She planted her foot in the middle of my chest, and slammed me seven feet up and into the water." BJ spluttered, "Is she into martial arts or something, because I can call quits on the damn gun."

Victoria smiled. "She's my bitch of an *ex*-girlfriend. My current bitch of a girlfriend is just about to destroy your family business. Watch and learn how corporate piracy works."

BJ and Victoria stood side by side in the wildly swaying little boat. They watched the mad scramble to abandon the burning sloop. BJ anxiously scanned the mayhem, trying to locate Ginette. Victoria too stood tense with worry.

"I can't see her through the damned smoke," BJ growled, and asked, "Is that a halyard line running from *Monster*'s mast top to Carmelo's boat?"

"I sincerely hope so."

A splash and angry shouts alerted them to Ginette's escape. Victoria spun the wheel to go collect her. Even as they moved forward, an unholy creaking scream rent the air as *Green Eyed Monster* shifted off the sandbar. She was now effectively being towed sideways by the high-powered pirate vessel, dragged mercilessly at a perilous tilt by the halyard rope attached to her mast top.

"Shit," shouted BJ, "they're pulling it down on top of themselves. Ginette's in the water. It'll land on her." She dove in the water, breaking into a punishing crawl, heading directly to a floundering Ginette, who had surfaced several yards away.

Green Eyed Monster had a very tall mast. The working lines or halyards that ran up and down it were much, much longer. As Carmelo's boat powered away, the line attached from *Monster's* mast top to his stern cleat snatched tight, slowing his vessel so abruptly, it stalled his engine. The powerful surge of the almighty tug managed to jar the sloop's long keel loose from the small groove it had made for itself in the soft sandbar. Victoria watched the sickening sway as it slowly swooned sideways.

All the groaning vessel could do was tilt toward the force hauling it. Had it been afloat in deeper water it would have drifted sideways, but perched on the semisolidity of a sandbank gave her keel a pivot point, and that allowed her to simply fall over onto the vessel dragging her down by her mast top. It was a harrowing ballet, but Victoria had to drag her eyes away and hunt through the waves and drifting red smoke for Ginette, and now BJ, who was in this melee, too.

❖

BJ cleaved through the waves until her head bobbed up behind Ginette's. She wrapped an arm around her chest and began to drag her away from the ensuing carnage.

"No, no, no!" Ginette screamed, splashing hysterically, nearly pulling them both under with her kicking and flaying.

"It's me, babe, it's me. Calm down. I got you." BJ soothed her, her strong backstroke pulling them both toward Victoria and the waiting powerboat.

"Oh, thank God, I thought you were a shark." Ginette twisted around and floated across BJ's belly, her tearstained face breaking into a huge smile. "I thought my karma had come to collect."

"Maybe it has." BJ smiled back.

They paddled backward together, grinning stupidly at one

another, lost in their own floating world until a voice above them said rather snidely, "Ahem, sorry to burst the love bubble, but is there any chance you two might climb onboard so we can get the hell out of here?"

All three sat at a safe distance and watched the terror of the men on Carmelo's deck as *Green Eyed Monster* slowly crept closer and closer to the hull of the motor cruiser. Sparks and flaming tatters of canvas were drifting across from the beleaguered vessel, along with blinding smoke. The rainfall of sparks had begun to singe and smolder on various fiberglass surfaces, the modern hull an even more flammable material. From the nearby island, high-powered rescue craft were already streaking toward the conflagration. Every boat in the vicinity had a camera leveled at the spectacle. It was cinematic in its high drama.

Ginette sighed happily. "Look at my beautiful creation. This must be how Shakespeare felt."

Finally, a crewman found the line that bound them to the burning hulk and hacked it away. Above, on the upper pilot deck, a practically apoplectic Carmelo was screaming at his helm to "Get the fuck outta here!"

But it was too late. *Green Eyed Monster* had passed the point of no return. She keeled right over to lie at ninety degrees, her beam resting on the sandbar. The surrounding waters hissed and steamed as they quenched most of the fire on her hull and deck. Freed at last from her blazing thirty-eight-foot anchor, the power craft shot forward for a speedy escape.

"Ooh, watch this," Victoria said. With a sickening thump and a grinding wrench, the expensive motor cruiser came to an immediate stop, as if it had hit an invisible brick wall.

"What the hell happened?" BJ asked.

Victoria smiled. "Current bitch of a girlfriend has been underwater winding a length of chain around their propeller while they were sitting stalled. Their engine has just jumped a piston, and these guys are going nowhere awful fast."

A large splash behind them heralded the return of the diver. Hauled quickly back onboard, Mickey stood and shivered in Victoria's arms as they all stood watching *Monster* lying on her side, smoking and sizzling as the last of the flames died out along her beautiful teak planking. Victoria cradled Mickey gently, realizing the shaking was mild shock at the death throes of her beloved boat.

"Oh." Mickey managed a small sad sigh. Victoria held her tighter, knowing her dreams were being slowly destroyed.

CHAPTER SIXTEEN

B J wiped the steam from her bathroom mirror. Finally, it had been her turn for the shower. Forever the perfect host, she had surrendered up her guest room, her bathroom, and copious amounts of hot water to her bedraggled comrades. Ginette had elbowed her way to the top of the waiting list claiming smoke inhalation, seawater in her hair, and uncharacteristic heroism as absolute musts for her to go first.

Victoria and Mickey had gone next under the guise that showering together would speed up the whole process. They took over an hour and left BJ's bathroom looking like SeaWorld after the dolphin show. But her guests were squeaky clean, with very smug smiles when they finally made their steam-filled exit.

Now a relaxed and well-scrubbed BJ strolled down the hall of her small bungalow to her bedroom, towel wound around her waist, briskly rubbing her damp locks. She smiled contentedly. Overall, it had been a good day. She had seen Carmelo and his amigos hauled away as a rescue quickly became an arrest. The narcotics found on his boat putting him in cuffs. BJ smiled at the memory. What a chump! He was so intent on coming after her and the rich American, in his greed Carmelo hadn't even bothered to offload Rudy's cargo.

Never before had BJ been so happy *not* to be mixed up with her uncle's other businesses. This kidnapping fiasco had been the exception to the rule, a deal accepted when she was flat broke and desperate. She knew she was very lucky to have gotten away as easily as she had. These women could have turned on her. Instead, she had the curious feeling she'd made friends through adversity.

She passed through the lounge where Victoria and Mickey bent over her computer talking babel, as far as she was concerned, about the mysteries of high finance and international money laundering. But her guests seemed content, and BJ smiled. Soon she would be a half millionaire. What a day. She was alive, Carmelo was arrested, and she was rich! She sniffed the air appreciatively. And apparently her new "wife" was cooking in her kitchen. Again, what a day.

Mickey nodded absently to her host as she wandered by seminaked.

"I'm glad BJ let us collapse here tonight. I need some serious rest before facing Rudy the reptile tomorrow."

Victoria looked up, her attention immediately drawn from the columns of figures on the screen before her to the striking body passing through. She silently watched BJ with considerable appreciation.

"Yeah, so much better than a hotel," she murmured absently.

"Hey." Mickey nudged with her shoulder. "Stop drooling."

"I can drool all I want. I'm a single woman. I'll wear a bib round my neck if I need to." Victoria sniffed. "It's none of your business."

"Well, stay away from the keyboard, in case your dribbling fuses the whole house," Mickey responded sourly. With a huff, she returned to her work. *Is this all it's going to be between us, then, just sex? Red-hot, gut-melting sex, and nothing else. I dreamed of more than that. If it had just been sex, I wouldn't wake every morning all eaten up inside.* She slid a sideways glance at Victoria. *I wonder what she dreams about. What she wants?*

❖

At the kitchen, BJ made a small detour to where Ginette stood at the stove checking on the contents of a stew pot. BJ enveloped her in a huge hug, burying her face in her neck, inhaling the wonderful essence of the woman as well as the food.

"Hey." Ginette squirmed but didn't pull away. "What do you think you're doing?"

"I'm squeezing my wife of the week." BJ smiled into the soft flesh just below the earlobe, kissing it with relish. "You still owe me a Glock 33. So I got a whole week of wifeyness to collect on," she teased.

"Speaking of guns." Ginette squirmed even more at the nibbling. "I knocked you overboard before Carmelo could shoot you, thereby saving your life." She managed to wriggle enough space to turn around in BJ's arms and face her. "That should make us even— Oh, my God. You're naked." Her palms were on the heated satin of BJ's rib cage, her gaze level with a broad chest. She felt her face uncharacteristically flush.

"No, I'm not naked. Not yet." One quick flick and the towel pooled around BJ's feet. She pulled Ginette closer, grinning widely, her eyes glittering mischievously.

"Stop it," Ginette protested weakly. "We're in the kitchen. It's unhygienic." Her Boston cool was steaming up like the gumbo. BJ continued to sway her in her arms.

"You were saying?" she continued to tease. "You saved my life by kicking my ass into a sea of flames, and that means what? We're even?"

Ginette smiled. "In some cultures it even means I own you."

"Indeed? Well, maybe so, Mrs. Jack, maybe so." BJ kissed her, long and slow.

BJ felt cocky, full of confidence for the way things would run with this attractive, completely mesmerizing American lady.

After all, they were both so sure of each other, had each other's measure from the moment they'd met. They recognized like for like. They were both players, with lives full of hot hellos and quick good-byes.

Several minutes later, they drew back from each other, both blinking and breathing erratically. What should have been a sexy, salacious kiss had dissolved into addictive, first-time sweetness. It left BJ with an instant buzz, but not a sex rush low in the belly as expected. Instead, this ache was higher up, a soft warmth that flowed through the heart and onto her flushed face.

"Hmm, when will dinner be ready?" BJ groped for something to say, clumsily pulling her towel back into place.

Ginette stood, silently watching BJ awkwardly right herself. She too had floundered at the pure, simplicity of the kiss. But Ginette was a pragmatist. Life had thrown her many learning curves recently, and she had fumbled and flunked each one in turn. Now here was another lesson, or trick, or obstacle. Hell, she had no idea what it was. She frowned quizzically at the woman before her. How could she be allowed to have any luck so soon after everything stupid, selfish, and downright evil she'd done? Why were her karmic lessons coming at her in unrelenting waves?

"Dinner?" She looked in those flummoxed midnight eyes, and saw her own questions staring right back at her. BJ was a bruised heart, too. Under all her bluff and bluster lay the belief she deserved little in life but could survive despite the odds. Maybe this was meant to be their time to be together, to learn and grow beside each other. Who knew? Ginette hated all this karmic crap.

Decision made, she turned off the stove. "Dinner won't be ready for a few more hours."

Her pale fingers interlaced with BJ's duskier ones as Ginette took karma by the hand and led it to the bedroom.

❖

"Done." Victoria clicked the shutdown icon. "We have saved the world as we know it."

"Saved your ass, more like." Mickey snorted. She removed her glasses from her tired eyes, still feeling out of sorts from BJ's earlier peepshow and Victoria's reaction to it.

"My ass, your world. What's keeping dinner?"

Mickey stretched and scowled. She'd had a very bad day. She had lost all her illicit millions in one fell swoop, to a ruthless and very sexy corporate pirate. So, no surprises there. She had also lost her holiday resort investment and witnessed the destruction of her adored yacht. *Didn't see that coming, did ya, hotshot? Didn't see any of it. She got you good this time.*

She sighed, resigned to the outcome despite her self-scolding. Her shoulders slumped as she watched Victoria wander off to the kitchen. Now she was losing her other green eyed monster, the one she'd named her boat after. The one she'd wanted to share her future with in one form or another, whether flesh and blood or oak and teak. Panic rose. Now she'd lost them both. *Now you're really sinking.*

Victoria was correct that she was a single woman. A successful, rich, corrupt, single woman who could ogle any big spunky butch she fancied. Mickey had nothing to offer her, never really had. She was good at taking, but had nothing to give. She glanced up from her self-pitying reverie as Victoria returned from the kitchen.

"Where'd they go? The kitchen's empty and the stove's not even turned—" Just then an orgasmic cry echoed from BJ's bedroom. Victoria's eyes widened and then crinkled as a delighted smile crossed her face. She raised her eyebrows at Mickey, who ruefully rolled her eyes.

"That answer your question?" Mickey answered flatly. "You'll have to make do with a sandwich."

Victoria drew closer, watching Mickey intently. "What's up with you? Aren't you happy for them?"

Mickey shrugged. "Sure I am," she replied indifferently.

"Then why so glum?"

"Oh, let me think. There must be something. Ah, I know what it is. Yesterday I was a multimillionaire, living on a beautiful Caribbean island, just messing round all day long on my classic yacht…then you came."

Victoria shrugged. "So you were happier yesterday. You gotta roll with the blows, Mickey. I've had to broker a deal to repay my back taxes. Your shenanigans brought a lot of heat down on me. I had to act fast. I sold my shares in my own companies before there was even a whisper of an investigation. And I'm nearly all paid up." A small smile tugged at her lips at the confession, "Believe it or not, I think at this very moment in time I may possibly be an honest citizen. And this evening I believe part of me is happier than I've ever been. I have a whole new, terrifying future lying ahead of me, and it makes me feel strangely excited." Mickey's jaw dropped in shock at her revelations. "Yup, you heard right. I am now officially broke. The money we've just recouped is all for the taxman. Everything changes, Mickey. Here today, gone tomorrow."

"Yeah. Sure seems so." Mickey gazed into her eyes and knew she was going to lose her again. Lose her to this terrifying and strangely exciting future that Victoria seemed so ready for. Holding on to Victoria Gresham was as elusive as diving into the color of her eyes in the warm Caribbean waters. Mickey was always going to come up empty-handed.

Victoria watched Mickey closely, trying to ascertain the thoughts behind the sad, lost look. She wondered if she'd guessed right, or if once again she was falling for Mickey's smoke and mirrors. Was there a chance for them now that she was bankrupt, or was she going to end up alone, bereft of everything? What were her actual chances, now that she'd admitted that she was penniless to the woman who had always seen her as a commodity?

She understood Mickey's drive, her lust for the green dollar bill. Victoria let her shoulders sag in defeat. Mickey would most likely move on to the next good scam or dodgy deal, always looking for fast money and lots of it. It took a lot of hard work and commitment to get rich, either the good way or the bad, and twice as much to stay that way. Mickey would have to move on quickly.

"Sometimes, some things stick," she said carefully, gently placing a hand on Mickey's shoulder. She was compelled to ask for an answer she was afraid to hear.

"Like…" She searched her mind quickly for an analogy. "Like barnacles." She winced. *What the hell am I trying to say here?*

"Barnacles? You calling me a barnacle?"

"No, no. *I'm* the barnacle. Well, no, I'm not… That was a bad analogy. Forget it."

"*You're* the barnacle?" Mickey's eyebrows rose and the dimple deepened.

"I was thinking about the boat," Victoria defended hotly, annoyed at her crummy word selection. Why couldn't she have said albatross or dolphin or something? Mickey cocked her head. Her hands came up to span Victoria's waist. Victoria absently ran her palms down Mickey's firm biceps and forearms, savoring the contours. She frowned and tried again. "I was thinking about you and your boat. Sailing the seas."

"Aaah." Mickey nodded wisely. "And you're a barnacle."

"I'm *not* a barnacle. It was a bad analog—"

"You're the boat," Mickey interrupted.

Victoria blinked, confused.

"You're the boat," Mickey continued to explain. Her grip tightened. "You're the *Green Eyed Monster.* I named her for you. I wanted to sail away with her. Sailing lifts my heart. It's the closest I've been to happy since, well…since you."

"You think of me as a monster." Victoria was shocked; her mind reeled at the boat being named for her. Somewhere she sensed a compliment, of sorts.

Mickey nodded solemnly. "Always. Abominable, devilish, crazy, but always *my* little monster. I love you, Victoria." Sudden urgency entered her words now that they were out in the open.

"Victoria, stay with me. You're penniless. You'll starve. You can't cook, or shop with coupons, or do any poor people stuff." The grip on Victoria's waist tightened as Mickey continued her imploring. "Let's be poor together. I'll look after you. I'm good at poor. We can rent a place. Small and cozy, for just the two of us. We can be beach bums, and I can get a job in a bar...or a kitchen. Anything. You can even go to hairdressing college. Just...please don't go away. Think about it. Please, just think about it. I love you so much. I don't think I could bear losing you again."

Victoria stood stunned as Mickey's words sank in. This woman, like so many others before her, had only entered her life for her money. Now at her lowest ebb, empire relinquished, funds depleted, barely slipping out from the shadow of jail, now she was being offered the only thing she ever really wanted?

Finally, as a derelict, penniless beach bum, she was to be loved for herself? Her own bad-tempered, monstrous self? She stood incredulous of the real riches Mickey was pouring on her.

In a choked voice, she answered, "I can't leave...I'm a barnacle."

CHAPTER SEVENTEEN

The telephone shrilled out one ring before being silenced. It awoke Victoria out of her sleep long enough to register her growling stomach. She shifted out from under Mickey's heavy arm and pulled on a large T-shirt before she padded off in search of a late-night snack.

The ding of her microwaved meal enticed Ginette to the kitchen, too. She yawned and reheated another bowl of gumbo for herself and sat companionably with Victoria to eat.

"What time is it?"

"Hmm, around four o'clock, I think. Who was on the phone?" Victoria asked.

"BJ's brother warning her to lie low. Rudy has been arrested on narcotics charges. Seems Carmelo has been squealing like a stuck pig for a police deal."

"Is BJ going to be all right?"

"Oh, yes. She had nothing to do with their drug running. She was only drafted in to work in the 'kidnap, torture, and murder you' project."

"Thank goodness for that," Victoria drawled.

Ginette seemed unperturbed. "And since that never actually happened, and Rudy never reported his boss's abduction, she's totally safe. There never was a kidnapping as far as the authorities are concerned. Rudy is hardly going to confess to one, now is he?"

"You like her, don't you?"

"Yes. I'm thinking I might blackmail her into sticking around."

"Blackmail?"

"Yes. Some people have happily ever after, we'll have blackmail. *Comme ci, comme ça.*" They ate a few more spoonfuls in silence.

"What about you?" Ginette asked.

"Me?"

"Yes, you and whatsherface."

"Ah, we don't have blackmail. We have 'You're penniless and you're mine.'"

"Bankruptcy." Ginette nodded slowly in appreciation. "That works, too, I suppose."

"Plus, I love her."

"I know." Another companionable silence, which Ginette broke. "So, what are you gonna do about it? Stay here? Take her back with you? What?"

Victoria contemplated this and shook her head. "I'm not sure what will happen, or what lies ahead for us. I only know the one thing she ever wanted to do was run away on that stupid boat. What about you?" Victoria asked. "You and BJ seem…cozy." *Understatement of the year. Hyenas mate more quietly.*

"When I'm around her, I feel sort of stalked."

"Stalked?"

"Yes, I think love and karma are out to get me."

Victoria smiled. "Wow, that's a pretty mean tag team, Ginette. You want to be careful there. Think you and BJ can take them on?"

Ginette shrugged, her face totally open and honest. "Well, I think I pretty much got karma's moves covered. But love, well, I'm not so sure about that. No offense to our relationship or anything, Vic. I do love you, but as a friend, and I probably always loved you like that, even when we were together." She looked directly at Victoria. "It's just that, well, I'm realizing I don't know a thing about the heart-stopping, gut-churning sort of love. So I'm not sure what to expect. And I'm not too crazy about the lack of control that goes with it. Hence the blackmail. I can make BJ stay or go, depending on how scared I get."

"You look at things very uniquely, Ginette. Blackmail, kidnap, arson. You've added a whole new chapter to the *Ways to Say I Love You* handbook. And for the record, we had fun together, we were good, and you'll always be my friend. I think you've got a better handle on love than you realize. You don't need it to coerce BJ to stay or go. I've seen the way she looks at you. I think she has her own ideas about what she wants."

"Thank you." Ginette nodded her head and chewed thoughtfully. "When do I get my money?"

Victoria smiled at her directness. "Later. We'll talk about that with BJ at a more godly hour." She stood up to rinse her dish and go back to bed. With a light kiss on the top of Ginette's head she murmured, "Sleep tight, sweetheart."

❖

"No, no, please. I can't take any more. You've got to stop. You're killing me." Victoria gasped, her hands weakly pushing at the heavy head nestled between her thighs. "This can't be legal. It's assassination." She was drenched in sweat, her breathing coming in ragged heaves. All her limbs had melted under the carnal onslaught she'd just undergone. She rolled from her side onto the flat of her back to escape Mickey's attentions.

"I'm done in," she groaned. "I just can't multitask at this level."

Dawn was creeping through the window blinds, and her body felt as if she hadn't closed her eyes all night.

"Hey. This is supposed to be a sixty-niner. You haven't been keeping your end of the bargain. Where's your fifty percent, huh?" Mickey complained.

Victoria shook her head feebly. "Can't do math right now. Brain's turned to soup."

Mickey crawled up the bed and snuggled into her. "Okay, Soupy, but you owe me half a sixty-nine."

Victoria idly played with the long strands of dark blond hair, letting them run through her fingers like silken threads. "Are you making demands?"

"No demands. I'm calling it a debt."

"A debt for oral satisfaction?"

Mickey rolled onto her belly and languorously licked Victoria's nipple as if it were a blob of raspberry ice cream. She nodded in satisfaction at the entire situation. "Yes. You owe me oral satisfaction."

"Hmm. What if I just said something nice? Would that count?"

"Well." Mickey ceased her lazy licking and scrunched up her face in thought. "I suppose if you said you'd be my sex slave for a day, that might seal the deal."

Victoria sighed. She would obviously just have to manage the conversation herself. "What if I told you *Green Eyed Monster* was probably salvageable? At great cost, mind you, but salvageable."

Mickey's head popped up, hers eyes full of hope. She stayed silent. Victoria cleared her throat before continuing.

"What if we used the last of my honest money and got her shipshape again? And made her our floating home. Maybe even take a cruise, just the two of us. Sort of like a make-or-break honeymoon thingy."

Mickey gave a big blink at the word *honeymoon*. Misreading it, Victoria hurried on flustered. "Not honeymoon! I meant holiday. I mean if we can survive in a confined space for several weeks and not poison, drown, or stab each other, there's a pretty good chance that maybe we could hang out together. In the future, I mean."

"Hang out?" Mickey asked cautiously.

"Mmm, well, be together."

"Like a couple?"

"Yes, a couple."

"Who hang out together?"

"Well, yes, most couples hang out together. Hence the word *couple*."

"Who live together?"

"Yes, I suppose we would be living together. On the boat."

"Like partners?"

"Well, yes, maybe—"

"Like wifey and wifey?"

"That's a bit quick!"

"Like barnacle and boat?"

"Hey." All further protests were smothered by a big kiss from her intended.

CHAPTER EIGHTEEN

B J and Ginette sat and blinked in unison.
"You did what?" Ginette asked.

"Huh?" BJ managed.

That's so sweet. They even blink in harmony now. Victoria smiled patiently and explained again, for the third time. "We've signed over the resort to both of you. You have co-ownership."

"Where is my money?" Ginette demanded.

"In the resort," Victoria answered with growing impatience.

"And my half mill?"

She looked at BJ. "In the resort. What part of this don't you both get?"

"You've put all our money in that resort?" Ginette spluttered.

Finally. Victoria sighed in relief. "Yes. All the funds Mickey and I clawed back into legitimate American accounts have to go to pay excess fines and back taxes. There won't be much left after that. The resort is one of the few remaining unclaimed resources I have left to pay you with."

"That's not what we agreed." Ginette began to panic, her voice becoming slightly squeaky.

"Actually, we didn't agree on anything, just that I recompense you. And I've done that through real estate. Same goes for you, BJ. You can now take over from your uncle. May he rot in jail—sorry, I meant hell."

"Hey—" Ginette began to protest again, but Victoria held up her hands.

"It's done. Take it or leave it. Run it, sell it, demolish it, burn it to the ground. But it's yours, and it's a done deal. You both now own the resort. Go make it work."

As far as Victoria was concerned, the deal was closed, and it was for the best. No scams, no shortcuts, no blackmailing—she had given them both a fresh new start. *So, BJ, let's see how quickly your wife for a week turns into a future life together. And, Ginette, I think you've finally found your equal footing. You have your money, your lover, your new business. Go work that ass off, girl. I think it's about time you said hello to your heart.*

❖

"How'd they take it?" Mickey looked up as Victoria joined her on the dock.

"I left them bickering over percentages and who was the boss. That resort will be their glue in the first instance, until all the other things drop in place."

"And then what?"

"Then they'll wake up one morning and realize they're a forever type of couple."

"Just like us?"

"Just like us."

"What was our glue?"

Victoria grinned. "Your greed for my money."

"And here we are, waiting to see a man about a boat, so we can sail off into the sunset and live like ship rats. So what happened to our glue?"

"It's still there. It's just the nature of the greed has changed." Victoria rubbed a possessive hand over Mickey's belly as she snuggled in under her arm. "Now all I want is you."

Mickey smiled down at her. "Done deal. You got me, for

richer, for poorer. Now let's go see this guy about a salvage operation."

In the warm Caribbean sunshine, arms twined around each other's waists, they wandered down the jetty. Topaz water sparkled on either side. The breeze was balmy, and the sun shone down on them. They had each other and not much else. But sometimes empty pockets mean full hearts, and in that particular currency, they were forever rich.

About the Author

Gill McKnight has contributed short stories to the award-winning *Best Women's Erotica 2008* (Cleis Press), *Romantic Interludes 1: Discovery* (Bold Stroke Books), *Ultimate Lesbian Erotica 2009* (Alyson), and *Read These Lips: Openings.*

Her debut novel, *Falling Star*, was published by Bold Strokes Books in July 2008, followed by *Green Eyed Monster* and *Goldenseal* (forthcoming September 2009).

Books Available From Bold Strokes Books

Green Eyed Monster by Gill McKnight. Mickey Rapowski believes her former boss has cheated her out of a small fortune, so she kidnaps the girlfriend and demands compensation—just a straightforward abduction that goes so wrong when Mickey falls for her captive. (978-1-60282-042-5)

Blind Faith by Diane and Jacob Anderson-Minshall. When private investigator Yoshi Yakamota and the Blind Eye Detective Agency are hired to find a woman's missing sister, the assignment seems fairly mundane—but in the detective business, the ordinary can quickly become deadly. (978-1-60282-041-8)

A Pirate's Heart by Catherine Friend. When rare book librarian Emma Boyd searches for a long-lost treasure map, she learns the hard way that pirates still exist in today's world—some modern pirates steal maps, others steal hearts. (978-1-60282-040-1)

Trails Merge by Rachel Spangler. Parker Riley escapes the high-powered world of politics to Campbell Carson's ski resort—and their mutual attraction produces anything but smooth running. (978-1-60282-039-5)

Dreams of Bali by C.J. Harte. Madison Barnes worships work, power, and success, and she's never allowed anyone to interfere—that is, until she runs into Karlie Henderson Stockard. Eclipse EBook (978-1-60282-070-8)

The Limits of Justice by John Morgan Wilson. Benjamin Justice and reporter Alexandra Templeton search for a killer in a mysterious compound in the remote California desert. (978-1-60282-060-9)

Designed for Love by Erin Dutton. Jillian Sealy and Wil Johnson don't much like each other, but they do have to work together—and what they desire most is not what either of them had planned. (978-1-60282-038-8)

Calling the Dead by Ali Vali. Six months after Hurricane Katrina, NOLA Detective Sept Savoie is a cop who thinks making a relationship work is harder than catching a serial killer—but her current case may prove her wrong. (978-1-60282-037-1)

Dark Garden by Jennifer Fulton. Vienna Blake and Mason Cavender are sworn enemies—who can't resist each other. Something has to give. (978-1-60282-036-4)

Shots Fired by MJ Williamz. Kyla and Echo seem to have the perfect relationship and the perfect life until someone shoots at Kyla—and Echo is the most likely suspect. (978-1-60282-035-7)

truelesbianlove.com by Carsen Taite. Mackenzie Lewis and Dr. Jordan Wagner have very different ideas about love, but they discover that truelesbianlove is closer than a click away. Eclipse EBook (978-1-60282-069-2)

Justice at Risk by John Morgan Wilson. Benjamin Justice's blind date leads to a rare opportunity for legitimate work, but a reckless risk changes his life forever. (978-1-60282-059-3)

Run to Me by Lisa Girolami. Burned by the four-letter word called love, the only thing Beth Standish wants to do is run for—or maybe from—her life. (978-1-60282-034-0)

Split the Aces by Jove Belle. In the neon glare of Sin City, two women ride a wave of passion that threatens to consume them in a world of fast money and fast times. (978-1-60282-033-3)

Uncharted Passage by Julie Cannon. Two women on a vacation that turns deadly face down one of nature's most ruthless killers—and find themselves falling in love. (978-1-60282-032-6)

Night Call by Radclyffe. All medevac helicopter pilot Jett McNally wants to do is fly and forget about the horror and heartbreak she left behind in the Middle East, but anesthesiologist Tristan Holmes has other plans. (978-1-60282-031-9)

I Dare You by Larkin Rose. Stripper by night, corporate raider by day, Kelsey's only looking for sex and power, until she meets a woman who stirs her heart and her body. (978-1-60282-030-2)

Lake Effect Snow by C.P. Rowlands. News correspondent Annie T. Booker and FBI Agent Sarah Moore struggle to stay one step ahead of disaster as Annie's life becomes the war zone she once reported on. Eclipse EBook (978-1-60282-068-5)

Revision of Justice by John Morgan Wilson. Murder shifts into high gear, propelling Benjamin Justice into a raging fire that consumes the Hollywood Hills, burning steadily toward the famous Hollywood Sign—and the identity of a cold-blooded killer. (978-1-60282-058-6)

Truth Behind the Mask by Lesley Davis. Erith Baylor is drawn to Sentinel Pagan Osborne's quiet strength, but the secrets between them strain duty and family ties. (978-1-60282-029-6)

Cooper's Deale by KI Thompson. Two would-be lovers and a decidedly inopportune murder spell trouble for Addy Cooper, no matter which way the cards fall. (978-1-60282-028-9)

Romantic Interludes 1: Discovery ed. by Radclyffe and Stacia Seaman. An anthology of sensual, erotic contemporary love stories from the best-selling Bold Strokes authors. (978-1-60282-027-2)

A Guarded Heart by Jennifer Fulton. The last place FBI Special Agent Pat Roussel expects to find herself is assigned to an illicit private security gig baby-sitting a celebrity. (Ebook) (978-1-60282-067-8)

Saving Grace by Jennifer Fulton. Champion swimmer Dawn Beaumont, injured in a car crash she caused, flees to Moon Island, where scientist Grace Ramsay welcomes her. (Ebook) (978-1-60282-066-1)

The Sacred Shore by Jennifer Fulton. Successful tech industry survivor Merris Randall does not believe in love at first sight until she meets Olivia Pearce. (Ebook) (978-1-60282-065-4)

Passion Bay by Jennifer Fulton. Two women from different ends of the earth meet in paradise. Author's expanded edition. (Ebook) (978-1-60282-064-7)

Never Wake by Gabrielle Goldsby. After a brutal attack, Emma Webster becomes a self-sentenced prisoner inside her condo—until the world outside her window goes silent. (Ebook) (978-1-60282-063-0)

The Caretaker's Daughter by Gabrielle Goldsby. Against the backdrop of a nineteenth-century English country estate, two women struggle to find love. (Ebook) (978-1-60282-062-3)

Simple Justice by John Morgan Wilson. When a pretty-boy cokehead is murdered, former LA reporter Benjamin Justice and his reluctant new partner, Alexandra Templeton, must unveil the real killer. (978-1-60282-057-9)

Remember Tomorrow by Gabrielle Goldsby. Cees Bannigan and Arieanna Simon find that a successful relationship rests in remembering the mistakes of the past. (978-1-60282-026-5)

Put Away Wet by Susan Smith. Jocelyn "Joey" Fellows has just been savagely dumped—when she posts an online personal ad, she discovers more than just the great sex she expected. (978-1-60282-025-8)

Homecoming by Nell Stark. Sarah Storm loses everything that matters— family, future dreams, and love—will her new "straight" roommate cause Sarah to take a chance at happiness? (978-1-60282-024-1)

The Three by Meghan O'Brien. A daring, provocative exploration of love and sexuality. Two lovers, Elin and Kael, struggle to survive in a postapocalyptic world. (Ebook) (978-1-60282-056-2)

Falling Star by Gill McKnight. Solley Rayner hopes a few weeks with her family will help heal her shattered dreams, but she hasn't counted on meeting a woman who stirs her heart. (978-1-60282-023-4)

Lethal Affairs by Kim Baldwin and Xenia Alexiou. Elite operative Domino is no stranger to peril, but her investigation of journalist Hayley Ward will test more than her skills. (978-1-60282-022-7)

A Place to Rest by Erin Dutton. Sawyer Drake doesn't know what she wants from life until she meets Jori Diamantina—only trouble is, Jori doesn't seem to share her desire. (978-1-60282-021-0)

Warrior's Valor by Gun Brooke. Dwyn Izsontro and Emeron D'Artansis must put aside personal animosity and unwelcome attraction to defeat an enemy of the Protector of the Realm. (978-1-60282-020-3)